AK
20.12.06

A White Horse Publications Book

First published in Great Britain by White Horse Publications in 2006; this edition published by White Horse Publications in 2006

ISBN-10 095548040X ISBN-13 978095540409

Cover image © Chris Lowe and Chris Goodier 2006. Used with permission.

White Horse Publications is an independent literary agency and publishers. Contact them at feedback@whitehorsepublications.co.uk as they'd love to hear from you. Please recommend this book to a friend as they'd be very grateful.
www.whitehorsepublications.co.uk

before the eyes of the gods

ADAM KIRKMAN

dedicated to

everyone who ever broke my heart
(even if they never knew)

JC

'As flies to wanton boys are we to the gods,
They kill us for their sport.'

King Lear IV.i.38-9

THE GODS

JUPITER	supreme god
NEPTUNE	lord of the sea, also god of earthquakes and horses
VENUS	goddess of love
MINOS	god of wealth and the underworld
HELIOS	sun and the god of sun
APOLLO	god of youth, music, prophecy, archery and healing
THE ONEIROI	Morpheus, Phoebetor, Phantasos The Oneiroi are dream gods, children of Nox (the goddess of the night) and Somnus (the god of sleep)

THE PLAYERS

ARICIE	adopted, parents unknown
ANEURIN	son of Theseus and Hippolyte
PHÈDRE	daughter of Minos, grand-daughter of Helios
THESEUS	self-appointed Champion of Neptune

7

prologue

(nineteen years previously)

Swoop in low over rainforest; sound of heavy breathing stifled. She must keep her child quiet; too much noise will give away where she is, may the gods help her! She is tired, too tired, so tired; maybe she could rest her head, here, for a few minutes, on this rock, behind those trees.

And that's where they found her: such a proud woman, a queen nonetheless, but just another mortal soul to have shuffled from this immortal planet. Drawn by the sound of the baby crying, she is discovered near dawn by the search party who have been tracking her since she left the harem, for she alone among the enforced and the enslaved was unfortunate enough to conceive.

She wasn't even his favourite: he couldn't even remember her among the rest, but her child was his, and what was his stayed his. This child had a future, was something special. She remembered him though, the brutal heartless man – his whims, carried out so speedily and efficiently by sycophantic subservients – the phallocentric womaniser, harking back to the medieval days of a wench from every town. He wanted Brazilian flesh, Brazilian breast, the warm womanly smell of a wild Brazilian woman, and his whims were met.

Hunting parties, employed on a hush-hush basis, traversed the Amazon rainforest to find some suitably nubile, suitably unknown, suitably wild women for him – after all, he was the King of Greece, and only visiting for a while, and they needed the money while they could grab it from the rich pervert.

Most of the search party had been the hunting party (good men are so hard to come by, quiet loyal men so much worse) and could remember this one, she had been vicious. Bathing in a stream, they had taken her by surprise. She screamed in incomprehension, but then they all did – she was taken to the seedy palace where the conquest would be made. She was strong, all right, the men remembered that – but what was more striking about her was her one breast, the other cleaved straight off. She was an Amazonian, a fierce hunter woman, still living in a tribe in the jungle in this age of television and buy one get one free offers. That's how they were sure it was her: that, and the newborn baby, covered in blood and screaming, held at her remaining breast.

When she had escaped he was still body bound, but now he had haemorrhaged from her, tiny baby fists grabbing, pulling on the way out, refusing to emerge alone and bringing too much with him. Maybe the birth would have killed her anyway, but the escape didn't help. She was dead and her baby, her precious baby, destined to rule her tribe, was taken from her. All she wanted was to protect him, her life force, her heir, her son.

A cold arm still clutched his writhing body.

A river trickled past, oozing lifelessness.

A man coughed, shifting nervously.

The arm was removed, and the baby picked up. Then, feeling guilty, the men left her corpse (bestial, naked, bloody) to the jungle, and went back. She was, after all, only a savage, and they had what they came for – Aneurin, son of Theseus, heir to the throne of Greece.

1

Sitting quietly beside a river at low tide, knees drawn up to his chin in foetal desperation for warmth. A cold day in London, the fog blanketing the distance like cataracts. He does not care, staring forth at the Thames with a disillusionment he could not shake. Misery seeped his existence, and his breath froze in the air, and he thought about why he suddenly felt so empty. He wasn't suicidal, he realised with a relieved glance at his wrists, attempting the self-pitying pleasure of imagining himself dead. Who would come to his funeral? Would they cry? Who would be drunk, would there be press, would it be private? But he didn't want this pit of pleasure, and resolved to move out from the fug of lethargy that descended onto him.

Sweeping orchestral score; a maelstrom of dream-like collages float around him, strings muttering delicately (harmonically) to themselves, effortlessly effervescent. Mournfully chilling and plaintive. He looked out at the river, and saw the bare shores exposed to the naked eye, themselves appearing somehow unsheathed, nude. All the stones and stories under the river suddenly came out to play, a wrecked shopping cart (students), a sodden disused pier (a throwback to better times), graffiti on the far wall (punk kids). The scene was unsettling. He didn't know why, but there was something fantastically empty and desolate about the low tide – how a waste land was revealed twice a day, but covered with exuberant life the rest of the time. And how pointless it was. That a stone spent its life underwater, being slowly scraped away and into nothingness, its only break from the monotony of its existence was an airing to the skies, which would piss rain on it or send birds to shit on it.

'Fucking cheerful, I know,' he said, to no-one in particular. He got up from the pavement where he had been sitting, only just noticing the slight drizzle, and strode back towards the Tube, turning down a street where the drain had blocked, leaving him to leap in a balletic pose from dry patch to dry patch. He was momentarily distracted by a flickering blue light spark into existence in a top floor window in one of the nearby flats – a minor deity, he thought, and this was confirmed when a child's giggles shone piercingly into the urban gloom.

Tonight's dinner was a social function, he wasn't exactly sure what. He was sure it would be the usual suspects of dignitaries (all of whom ironically have no dignity…the tales he heard from servants) to whom he must be polite, so smarmingly polite, oh yes, really? No! whatever did you do next? Ah, yes, the political climate is tough, especially with Jupiter in such a mood! He wasn't sure how much more he could take, particularly in his advanced state of lethargy.

Oh the miseries of teenage life! The fact he knew he was typically teenage didn't help him overcome his pubescent problems; the disaffection; the irritation; the calculated antipathy. But recently, he'd been fine, which was why his sudden misery struck him so painfully. Since coming to London to study Essil (the language that came before the gods) at

University he'd been fine, it had done him good to get away from his family and his home. There was something undeniably uncomfortable about achieving adulthood under your childhood roof, something that nagged at the corner of your mind like bass rhythms in a tinny speaker. Present, but unheard. He didn't really mind his dad all that much, and – come to think of it – he didn't really mind his mother all that much, either.

She wasn't his real mother, of course, he had never known her. But his dad's wife seemed to have a problem with him, and had made his life a living hell back in Athens. Still, she seemed to have got her way, and with typical feminine manipulativeness, she had dispatched him overseas to study. Phèdre, finally free of him, got her wicked way with the King.

2

Aneurin liked his dad: apparently, he had been a bit wild in his youth, but when you're young and you have money in your pocket and power in your voice, you're likely to do anything. He knew how the blood burns. Not that it excuses anything, he thought, but at least Aneurin could sympathise with his father. He knew what it was like to be placed under the charm of women. Besides, since Aneurin's birth, Theseus had been a model citizen – not just to the media, but also in reality. Fatherhood made him grow up, and the change was not unnoticed: a slow shift in popularity accompanied his slow shift to decency. In many ways, he was unlucky that the thing that made him happiest was somehow connected to his tragic past.

He hadn't known it at the time, but the truth revealed itself (as it always does through the construct of lust.) It would hardly have been polite to introduce her as sister to his first wife. Safer, much, to give her her own sparkling name: Phèdre. The name itself seemed sensual, breathed off the tongue, with post-coital softness and devotion.

Aneurin remembered when they met: it had not been all that long ago, really, and something about their encounter stuck in his mind. He pondered what it was. She had seemed awkward and on edge: but that was understandable given her desire for Aneurin to like her. Meeting prospective step-children contained all the self-doubt, fear and loathing as a first date after months of loneliness and isolation.

Perhaps it was how, when they met, she turned her feet slightly inwards, giving her an uncomfortably round-shouldered appearance that didn't suit her elegant, slim body. Maybe it was the blood-red hue that coloured her face when their eyes met, and the way in which she kept flickering her eyes towards Theseus as if seeking his approval.

Thinking about it now, he wasn't sure if he'd made eye-contact with her since that meeting. Maybe once. At the wedding.

It was fair to say he liked her: she seemed pleasant, and she made his father happy. That was enough for him, but things got complicated after the marriage. The baked meats did coldly furnish the wedding buffet. A crystal glass was approaching three-quarters full of amber champagne. The happy couple swung in each other's arms as their rings on their fingers glinted. The public outroar at the break with tradition, for a King to remarry, and especially to make that vow outside the Vault of the Gods, was tempered by Aneurin's public blessing of the ceremony. If the child with legal primogeniture rights had no problem with the union, why should the public? But six weeks later, Aneurin was in London, his head somewhat spinning at the course of events.

Home was a small basement flat. His father had wanted something more grandiose, but Aneurin liked to keep things small: save the big things for dreams. He spent all his days dreaming and his nights awake, too consumed by his own thoughts to sleep and too tired to make his daydreams a reality. (an all action plan never put into practice.)

Aneurin liked wiling time away looking at people's ankles as they passed on the street above his flat, finding something beautiful in the stories they told, and the tales he made up for them. Those heels? An important client…odd socks? An unorganised bank clerk…shoelaces untied? A fashion statement. There was something comforting about these tales, particularly when he made them up from his underground bunker. Safety. Snug. He got back and let himself in, inadvertently kicking the pile of junk mail into a scattered mess. Somewhere in that pile were directions for tonight's social.

First things first, though, he thought. There's only one way to really get through this evening: he slid on polished floors into his room, slipped a special CD into his equipment and sat on the floor between his audio paraphernalia, which loosely resembled two speakers.

The music started to play, and something unusual happened. As the sound waves burst forth from their metallic enclosures, they became visible, as if some amber particle hung upon them. Like dust caught in sunlight, the sound dances to Aneurin and settles on, saturates him. Aneurin breathes in this dust of the gods, having invoked Apollo, the god of music, and achieves a state of mind he can only describe as coloured blue. He experiences music, lost in the masturbatory act of musical appreciation, but remains guilt-free because of the pleasure he knows the traveller, whom he sometimes meets, derives from their meeting. He lets his mind wander: blue, green, empty, khaki. Blue. States of mind consume him. He worked out that perfection equalled (state of mind) x ((visual input) + (audial input))

e.g.

(confusion) x ((moonlight on + (mockingly triumphant
frosty fields) pre-chorus))

With this realisation, he began to swim; he imagined himself trapped between the atoms in a violin string (those emotional teases) but soon realised he wasn't trapped between atoms but between worlds and the vast interplanetary spaces became him, and all he knew was he had to consume the electrons orbiting these planet-atoms. He met someone, another traveller like himself, and with an epic ambience roaring into existence around him, he spoke:

> I SAW A MAN PURSUING THE HORIZON;
> ROUND AND ROUND THEY SPED.
> I WAS DISTURBED AT THIS;
> I ACCOSTED THE MAN.
> "IT IS FUTILE," I SAID,
> "YOU CAN NEVER –"
>
> "YOU LIE," HE CRIED,
> AND RAN ON.

He bid him adieu, my liege!

For some reason, he felt this traveller was important, to be revered, perhaps even worshipped, and he showed him the respect he deserved. He never spoke, but Aneurin knew him to be a traveller. From where he came, Aneurin did not know; nor did he know why he was visiting this world, why he worked his power through music, why he made Aneurin's state of mind ocean blue using the dust of the gods. Their dust couldn't be manipulated.

Aneurin had no control over what he said to the being, this power, but every time he spoke, he died, and every time he awoke from his hallucinogenic stupor, he was reborn.

He continued his journey – but this was a travel of reality, he rued as he showered and dressed smartly, but at least the rest of the evening's pleasantries should pass a bit quicker. Hey, maybe Aricie had been invited too – that would make the evening less of a waste of time.

Aneurin paused at the door to check the address where he was heading towards: he'd have to get the Tube to Maida Vale, then a taxi from there. He left, heading back up the stairs to rejoin the bustle of existence, a brisk breeze clearing his mind slightly as he turned the corner at the end of the road.

Back at the apartment, attention shifts to a now ringing phone, and the overly bulky answering machine. A woman's voice (concerned, out of breath, tearful):

'Ani? Are you there? Aneurin? Pick up…something terrible has happened…'

3

He knew straight away that something was wrong.

4

Aneurin arrived at the restaurant slightly later than he was supposed to – fashionably so? – and was surprised not to see anyone he recognised immediately. Everyone seemed to be sitting down, and there were no large parties. Who was he here to see? And where were they? He should really have read the invite more carefully.

'You made it, then,' a sweet voice whispered full frontal into his ear. Spinning around, a smile broke out on his face.

'Aricie – hey, where is everyone?'

He gave her a quick peck on the cheek – he felt brave to do so – and he thought he felt his heart stop. A deep pang of heat coursed through his ribcage, and he felt the depression-weight cauterise his breath, a sharp intake of pleasure and discomfort. She smelled stunning. She smiled back, a seductive curl of her lips throwing a jewelled beauty across her face.

'This is everyone. I thought you could do with a break. You've seemed a bit strange these past few days, and I thought a quiet meal out would relax you a bit.'

She looked up at him, eyelids flicking themselves back to reveal deep oases of brilliant green, pools of gladed water in which he longed to swim. He hoped his own eyes didn't betray how much he wanted to see those eyes open next to him, to wake up beside her in the morning, even if nothing happened the night before, just so he could see the exact moment her mind stumbles into consciousness and brightens the world. He imagined her half-opening an eye and him there, beside her, and – still slumbering – her moving closer to him, placing an arm across his chest and mumbling something incomprehensible into his shoulder.

'Maybe you can even tell me what's up.'

Again that smile, and she led him to their table. For two. Near this fake marble pillar, which melded black and white in some labyrinthine fractal pattern. They sat down, and Aneurin felt a sudden surge of nervousness that spasmed somewhere in his lower colon.

Conversation was delightful initially: the dainty flirting, the random talk, the attempts at impressing each other with wit and intellect. ('Why aren't strawberries the colour of straw?') Aneurin always felt that the onus was on him. He felt crushed under his own feeling of inadequacy. Soon, however, the banter died down, and the bottle of red wine began to take effect, and talk turned more serious.

'I noticed you'd been a bit, well, distant, lately…which is why I arranged this.'

She flashed a smile up at him. He felt he could trust her.

'Thanks, it's beautiful.'

Just like you.

'So, I'm wondering…want to talk about it?'

He supposed he'd better talk about it. He supposed he was just getting to know her – just getting to like her – and he had a lot of emotional baggage that he didn't think it fair to put on her without her knowing what she was getting into first.

He longed for a long lazy winter night where they lay entwined in each other's arms and told each other dark secrets and formed a close bond from which love would grow.

'Yeah. Er…where to start?'

'How about the beginning.' She caught his eye. 'Let's talk about your dad, and Phèdre.'

'That obvious, huh?'

'Only to me, to someone who knows you. You seize up when someone mentions her name. You're tense now.'

He realised that she was right, and made a conscious effort to relax. Aricie watched his shoulders sag and realised he looked pretty cute when he finally wound down a little.

'That's better.'

'Yeah. Sure is.'

He took a deep breath again. Was he really going to lay his insides bare to someone who could hurt him so much if he let her?

'It's not a publicised fact that Phèdre is Ariadne's sister.'

'Ariadne? Who's that?'

Aneurin thought for a second.

'I didn't realise that information was so secure too. She's my dad's first wife.'

'Your mother?'

'No. I never knew my mother…but I did know Ariadne.'

'You sound bitter.'

'It's not my bitterness. It's my dad's. We're very similar, you know. I think he's bitter because he treated her so badly…'

'What happened?'

Aneurin took a deep breath. It was long and complicated, but he wanted her to know.

'It was just after Dad became Champion of Neptune. He'd been away clearing pirates off Neptune's shores when his own father died suddenly and unexpectedly. He suddenly inherited the Championship, as primogeniture law states, and wasn't prepare for the power of it. Others were, however.'

'What do you mean?'

Aneurin paused to take a sip from his glass.

'He met a girl who helped him escape from prison, when the King of Crete took him as a political prisoner. Everything happened so quickly. Quicker than Phèdre,' he rued. 'They married in the Vault, but shortly –'

'The vault? Ani, this doesn't make sense. What is the vault? It doesn't sound very romantic!'

'It's the Vault Of The Gods. All my family marry there...it's said if anyone lies in there, they will be struck down instantly by the gods. It's a sort of mystical pre-nuptial agreement...'

Aricie smiled at the attempt at a joke.

'To have married there means their love was true, but I wonder how much the gods had to do with it. It is not a coincidence that a Champion of Neptune married a slave to Venus.'

'Slave?'

'Not willingly. But once Venus thought it time, she turned their marriage sour. Ariadne tried to kill Dad while he slept. She failed, and he had her imprisoned on Naxos. It's better than the death penalty!' he added, seeing the look on Aricie's face.

'It's not that,' she said. 'I've heard tales...her songs...she puts the Sirens to shame.'

The subtext hung in the air. The gods are cruel.

'I'm more concerned with the Vault Gods.' It was Aneurin who broke the silence. 'They have unlimited power, and it resides only in music, only within the underground vault where it plays.

'I've heard the music. It sounded angry that love they had

approved had been soured. They sounded pissed off. They'll be doubly vigilant about what is sworn there now.'

The subtext was still there.

There was a pause as they realised the horrific nature of the discussion. Aneurin silently, inwardly, cursed Venus. Aricie appeared to read him.

'You say Venus had something to do with this? Is that true, or the usual media bullshit?'

'I think it's true. There is a history – Phèdre's mother was struck down with an unholy passion for a bull.'

'A bull?'

'It's the stuff the internet was made for. But – with perverse realism – the union was blessed.'

'Blessed? Jupiter…the Minotaur?'

'They're a fertile race. I guess he's technically my nephew. Was.' Referring to Theseus' destruction of the tortured soul. [1]

'But we're getting off the point. Phèdre's mother was cursed by Venus with a passion for a bull. Phèdre's sister was cursed by Venus with a destructive passion for my father. Phèdre…'

'Yes?'

'Don't you see the pattern? You know how the gods work. It can only be a matter of time before Phèdre is struck down by some destructive passion. I fear for Dad. He survived Ariadne…but can he survive Phèdre?'

'What makes you so sure Phèdre will be struck down by Venus? She hasn't been the most powerful of gods for a while, the papers say she is waning.'

'I think she is planning something big to reawaken herself as a deity of power. I think there is something tragic coming. I feel it in music.' Aricie knew about his habit. She had dabbled herself occasionally, socially. 'And I think Phèdre is the key.'

---

[1]   For an account of the Minotaur's existence, see Appendix B – from *The House Of Asterion* by Jorge Luis Borges. (*Labyrinths*, 1964)

'Why Phèdre?'

'Because Venus has a vendetta against her family.'

'Couldn't it just be coincidence?'

'No, sweetie.' He smiled at her. She appeared unphased by the compliment. 'Phèdre comes from a family that descended directly from Helios. He is her grandfather.'

'Oh…now I see…Venus is pissed at him 'cos he revealed her affair to her husband…but why is she taking it out on his descendants? They had nothing to do with it, it's hardly fair.'

'The gods are hardly fair.'

The truth in the statement hung there for a second. Aneurin continued.

'So I think something bad is coming with Phèdre. Before I knew all this about her past, I thought she was good for Dad. She certainly made him happy, the happiest I'd seen him since Ariadne turned sour.'

'You're really close to your dad, aren't you?'

'Yeah. Which is why I'm surprised I'm here. But then everything about Phèdre is surprising. Take the wedding, for example. It was peculiar. It took place at the palace, which was unusual in itself.'

'Why?'

'As royalty, they would normally marry in the Vault.' A sparkle of understanding danced seductively in Aricie's eyes. 'But Dad had already sworn love there once – to do so again would be to invite death. They married in the throne room.'

'Actually, I think I remember…I saw a few black and white photos in the paper. And I saw you! I remember thinking you looked pretty cute…'

Yes! She thinks I look cute!

'But then I met you…and realised you weren't!' she laughed.

What? Is she joking? Is there truth in jest? How can she make my heart swell and then bleed inside a single beat?

'Seriously though, I would never had thought we would ever have met,' she continued, oblivious to Aneurin's mental sweat.

'And look at how horrible that turned out to be!' *I can play the whole friendly insulting game. Let's watch you squirm. Let's see your mental sweat.*

He realised he had overplayed it. There was an awkward silence.

He shifted uncomfortably, but she (thankfully!) gave him a get-out.

'So, the ceremony...' she prompted.

He launched himself into the story, full pelt, in an attempt to win her forgiveness. *Forgive me, please. (How pathetic am I?* a little voice asked.*)*

'It was so surprising. When the church guy said "you may kiss the bride" and the room exploded with flashes of bright white light bulbs, Phèdre and Dad kissed, but she kept looking at me, the whole way through, looking me right in the eye.

'That's weird, isn't it? And when we made eye contact, I could swear I heard some miserable music playing, even though the band hadn't set up yet. There was something in that eye contact. Like looking into the windows of the soul. And then she blushed, a deep scarlet colour.

'I didn't know what to do. I ignored it, it all felt a bit strange. But then six weeks later, Dad came and told me he and Phèdre had decided to send me to study the language of Essil overseas.'

'Essil? What's that?'

'It's not very interesting. It's the language used before the gods. It's to do with light and stuff – pretty boring. I have to learn it because Dad had to learn it, as his Dad had to, and his father before him...'

'I was going to study it at home, where the Royal Library has the greatest collection of books in Essil, but then all of a sudden I was sent here. It struck me as a little strange that it came out of the blue like it did – Dad and I had not discussed anything like it. I had been working hard on the language, and had been enjoying training my horses...'

'You like horses? Me too.'

'Yeah...I've got a certain skill with them, through Dad, and Neptune. I own two, who are superb beasts...Pegasus and Tristar.'

'What beautiful names.'

'Thanks. I had been spending my days training them, and then all of a sudden – bam!' He slapped a palm on the table. 'I find myself here, because of Phèdre. But here, of course, I met you.'

Aricie reached onto the table where his hand still lay. He was surprised at how her hand was cool to the touch, but that was probably because he had been uncontrollably flushing hot all through the evening. He felt as if he suddenly had too much blood in his body and needed to be a centimetre larger all the way round before he could feel comfortable with the extra blood. A little voice told him it was vasodilatation on the extremities of his skin. He told himself it was Aricie that was making him feel like this.

'I'll be here with you.'

She smiled at him again. The difference a smile can make. Aneurin suddenly realised for the first time since he'd met Phèdre things were suddenly better. It had been a relief to talk about it all.

And above all, it was gorgeous to spend time with Aricie, whose presence tonight seemed to ensure the sun would rise tomorrow.

'Thanks. I'll need you.'

They left the restaurant, and Aneurin invites her back to his apartment. He is enraptured when she says yes. Immediately his mind starts spinning as he over-analyses everything and the meaningless assumes meaning as the meaningful becomes irrelevant. He thinks that maybe something will happen, but maybe it will not.

Either way, he was going to tell Aricie that he loved her. There was really no use fighting it any more. He'd done that before: lied to himself and lied to her, lied about everything so he wouldn't have to face possible heartbreak. He'd chosen misery cried silently onto pillows at night alone rather than risk everything on the slim chance of reciprocation. But tonight felt different, felt special. He thought they were drawing close and he had a thousand thoughts in his head, all poetical declarations of love and potentialities of perfection, all one thousand thoughts thinking the same thing: he was falling for her so completely, and for once, he thought she might be falling for him.

He headed home with a spring in his step. His heart felt lighter. Phèdre and his father were hundreds of miles away. He was only really concerned with the girl on his arm as he flagged down a black cab and felt proud to be with her. Things were looking up.

5

I find myself descending through the heavy oak trapdoor hidden behind the dark red curtains that surround the throne. I know where this journey takes me, but I am prepared: a scarlet thread unravels from my pocket, tied around the brass ring on the surface of the door. Not many people know the door is there, but all have heard about what it contains. A labyrinth so vast it has been postulated that it is infinite, and with its mirrors, it may as well be. Space multiplied itself; fractalised itself; consumed itself; existed only to grow.

I know how this story is meant to go, but I find myself entering the maze, rather than my kin, as I have already seen. I am perplexed at this, and should be a little scared, but for some reason I am not. I descend the steps and take the hand of the man behind me, leading him down.

Dank dark infinite depths of steep stone steps, a heavy air settling a paranoia of wakefulness, or was it sleep, or somewhere in between where nightmares fleshed themselves into your mind, the Minotaur's home unsettled me, and my lover. But I pressed on, marvelling at the tunnels hewn from rock, lit with fluttering torches, admiring the mirrors placed opposite each other for limitless dreams, passing from room to room in this great hall, meeting nothing but a growing sense of consciousness becoming blurred. I know that while the Oneiroi ruled wakelessness, he had – should have – did have – no power here. Although I felt the usual rules did not apply here, I feared him not, because love drove me, protected me, was there in both sleep and wake, present in the day, and waking me at night just to hold me so I know I am wanted, and loved.

I knew, somewhere in reality, it had been my sister who had sent her man down here, armed with scarlet string against the blackness of human passion, but my love for my man was twice, thrice, immeasurably more, and it is I who am leading the way, bronze sword in one hand and my lover's, following, in the other. I journey deeper, unfearing, into the labyrinth, a mirrored catacomb of repression, determined to find the Beast of Passion, and smite him, and Venus, and destroy something of which she was proud.

I heard something akin to a roar. The voice was raw through unuse, and an inhuman melging forged in Venus' fiery furnace came into view. My man attempted to move forwards, but I pushed him back, and smote the Minotaur of Crete, cleaving his monstrosity from his shoulders, purifying him and my own race with a flexing of my muscles initiated by a chemical imbalance somewhere inside my cranium.

I turned. I breathed. I loved. A passionate clinch with my man in the darkness followed as we enjoyed the sensation of tongues meeting.

The scarlet thread lead back out, and we blinked heavily in the morning light, pupils contracting into beady nothingness. Saying nothing, I turn to my man, the man sent down to kill the Beast of Crete, the man who would wind his way through history to make some difference to the gesamkunstwerk, the man I loved, and tortuously admired, turned to him, moved to kiss him, turned to him, and as I turned, turned to gaze into his eyes, to see sun-swept fire reflected in his eyes, I turned – turned to see Aneurin.

She awoke in sweat, and the eroticism was close but fading. She had never felt so covered in shame, disgust and self-loathing.

6

He knew straight away that something was wrong. It had been a previously routine trip across the Atlantic, but as they approached the French coast dark storm clouds with a yellow tinge gathered and prepared to spit bile on them. The yellow tinge scared him. It meant there was god-dust in the clouds – a deity was entering the physical world, leaving behind the physical manifestations of their celestial breath, their heavenly will made into coloured dust. And the yellow?

He feared the god whose dust was yellow.

The plane lurched fearfully. Clouds had sprang from nowhere and seemed to be an expression of rage as they set about the craft, throwing it from side to side. Theseus was scared – scared that today might be his last, and the thought of his family without him was what really scared him.

It took little more than a glance through to the cockpit of the small plane to see worried looks on the pilots' faces. Theseus listened in.

'Where the hell did this storm come from?'

'I think that's it – hell. Do you know where we're being blown to?'

'Looks like…'

'La Rochelle.'

'The mouth of the Styx? The gateway to hell?'

'Yeah. Look at the cloud colour. They ain't natural. Some god is working this.'

'Shit…who? I'd say Neptune, but this yellow dust, and with him in the back…' He jerked his thumb towards Theseus, to whom Neptune was famously indebted.

'Yeah, I thought that too, and if it's not Neptune, it must be…'

'Shit. Jupiter.'

The terrifying thought hung there. Theseus looked out the window, fearing Jupiter but not death, and for a second he thought he could see a monstrous face etched into the yellow storm, twisted in malevolent rage and unadulterated anger. He fancied he saw muscles flex within the storm's flux, and the plane gave out a creaking noise – stress fractures began to form, and as the decompression slowly started, he was only dimly aware of his instincts stepping in and getting a parachute and an exit to work together to his advantage.

The next thing he felt was freefalling until a snapping jerk brought his senses back to the present. A rushing noise filled his ears. His limbs pulled him in all directions. The waves reached up for him, beckoning him into their watery arms. He had lost sight of the plane almost immediately, and had no idea what had happened to it.

His disorientation was complete as he was buffeted into the broken surface of the sea, and passed below the water line. Submerged, he had no idea which way was up. He thought he was drowning.

Water filled his lungs.

Theseus was drowning, and Jupiter's strength did not allow the turmoil to break. His control over the waters was so complete that natural laws bent and the bitter black night promised to be Theseus' last.

Just as Theseus breathed the last water into his lungs and felt the lactic acid burn his flagging strength, he felt the storm calm, and was elevated through the waters until he levitated above the choppy waves. All around him the storm raged, but he felt the water magically remove itself from his lungs, and pour out his mouth. He took a deep, rasping breath.

Before him stood Neptune, his craft of sea coral unaffected by the storm. Water was his domain, after all: as powerful as Jupiter was, Neptune's affinity with water meant he would always have some power.

'Welcome, Theseus. To the eye of the storm.'

He saw Theseus' bedraggled look of incomprehension.

'Jupiter may be the king of us, but I can bend his power. I have brought the eye of the storm here to save you. It is well known that I am indebted to you for clearing so many pirates from my shores. You are my Champion. I am here to pay that debt, to make good on my oath. The eye can take you to dry land, where you will be safe. Then we will be even.'

He studied Theseus' silent look with his own silence.

'If you do not wish me to repay my debt now, that is your choice. But I must warn you where you are. We are five miles from shore. You are elevated above the Seal of Styx, at the mouth of the river of the dead. You are on the gate to hell.

'Jupiter is a proud god, proud of the deities' traditions. He does not like it that I am indebted to you, a human. He hopes, in your death, to destroy the position of Champion and the use of the Mark. He wants you through the Seal and bathing in the Styx.

'But I can save you. Just say the word.'

By now, Theseus had caught his breath. Looking down at the

waves, he could see a metallic seal far below him, illuminated by Neptune's glowing presence. The Seal of Styx, he thought. The last great voyage.

Mankind had touched the stars, but had yet to touch the darkness of their souls.

'No.'

'No? I offer you life, and you choose death?'

'I fear Jupiter, but not death. I choose not to have you repay my debt yet. I will journey through the seal, and see the damned. I wish to see the banks of the Styx. And if your power is there, I may use it. If not, I will return. Now release me.'

'And what of your wife? Your son? Your unborn child?'

'Unborn child? What unborn child?'

'She has not told you yet, but a new king grows in her belly. Will you risk never seeing him, or any of them again?'

'I will see them again, I have no doubt of that. They are why I will return. And what a joyous reunion it will be.'

At these words, Neptune crackled into darkness and back into light.

'Now release me. I hope I do not need to call on you later.'

With that, Neptune relaxed his magical grip on Theseus, who plunged back into the water, which was once again whipped into waves of brutal strength. Somewhat prepared, Theseus held his breath and looked down on the Seal of Styx.

'Goodbye, Theseus. Fare thee well. I will see you again, soon.'

And with that, Neptune and all his brilliant light disappeared. Theseus could gauge where the seal was, and swam down to it in powerful strokes, but before long he could feel himself in a swirling vortex moving down towards the seal. He realised this powerful undercurrent was what was drowning him earlier, but now he relegated himself to its power and passed down to the seal.

His feet hit the metal, and he could see gouged script on its surface, but its language was foreign to him, and before he could memorise its minute form, his world was suddenly inverted as he found himself upside down, feet still on the seal, but now water was pouring past him towards the bottom of a cave so large and so dark it could have been infinite, and for all he knew, probably was. The sudden shock of the reversal of ground and sky – or water and seabed – caused Theseus to gasp, and he realised that there was air here, and he gratefully breathed in. He was still hanging by his feet as a waterfall rushed past and over him.

'What devilry…?'

He wondered out loud, and his voice penetrated only a few metres into the darkness. He thought he heard a response, but it was gone before it had registered properly. Already it seemed like a distant memory. Now, though, he realised the cave was not as dark as he first thought: an eerie phosphorous light shone dimly. He could see a river bank far below – above? – him, and he was not sure how to get there. Certainly he couldn't remain suspended upside down on this magic seal forever: the water rushing past him was cold, and the current was strong.

He felt sure Neptune was restraining its power. After all, the entire sea emptying through a metre wide magic hole would create enough pressure to blow him clean off the seal and crack his head open on the ceiling (floor?). He lifted one foot off the seal, and suddenly its hold on him was broken, and gravity reasserted itself, and he felt himself falling alongside the waterfall, but not in it, and he screamed, and then hit the ground.

The pain was sharp but soon went as Theseus escaped into unconsciousness.

He awakened some time later, but the scene was unchanged. He was beside a dark river that flowed with supernatural speed and strength. He could feel the presence of Neptune from the water, but there was something else present too: something so powerful that he had never felt before.

He felt it as some kind of music, if that's what the dissonant sounds could be called: it had a dreamy quality to it, but it was tonality fighting with atonality and the result was the sound of power made into sound. He was listening to raw energy, and it frightened him. Was this what lay beyond the world, in the darkness of human souls?

He sat up and looked about, investigating his surroundings. There was a wide bank upon which he sat, and he could see that there was just sheer cliff on the other side of the river. It was unclimbable, and probably reached up to the sloping ceiling at the cave's rooftop, and then all the way over a dizzying hundred and eighty degrees back to the wall behind him.

He was at the back of a cave, for the water poured out from the seal with devastating speed and gushed downstream to his right, and to his left there was nothing beyond the waterfall. He knew it was through Neptune's involvement that he had landed on the band rather than the river, landed alive rather than into death. From the look of where he lay, he thought no-one had ever been here alive before.

He only had one choice: to set off to his left, and head downstream alongside the Styx, the river of the dead. He set off, and felt something strange. Was it just the music, or his injured body addling his mind, or was time moving somehow differently down here?

He spoke out into the darkness.

'I am Theseus, King of Greece and Champion of Neptune. What is this place?'

He wished he hadn't spoken: a thousand bodies sat up from the river, screaming and cackling at him. They were all swept along at fantastic speeds, and he was safe from their clutching claws on the bank, but every now and then he caught the grotesque faces of the damned pouring past him.

He saw a child screaming racial and sexual obscenities at him, anger etched on her once innocent face. He saw mutilated bodies devouring each other, one holding his own detached mouth in his hand so he could reach around the woman he had dragged down with him and eat her from behind, as she screamed from the ragged bloody hole that had once been her mouth.

Everyone was covered with dirty mud, and each was screaming in mortal agony. His voice only penetrated a few metres as before, and was echoless, but the different movement of time in this place stretched it so it seemed to continue on for days and echo until he burst, and the snapshot of the damned lasted for a lifetime scratched into his memory. As Theseus' voice died, so the damned lay back below the surface, and were swept along in their silent agony.

He was shaken at the sight, and turned over to vomit the contents of his stomach up with a burning passion that flowed out his nose and mouth. He decided not to speak again, and set off down the river bank. So this was the Styx, and he was walking besides the river of death in a world where time moved differently, and travelling down into hell.

7

They entered the apartment, the pile of junk mail still scattered on the floor. Aneurin headed for the kitchen to switch on the kettle, while Aricie sat herself down on the plush white sofa. Palpitations suddenly seized him.

He glanced at her, and saw in a sudden sweep everything that could happen, all his emotional fantasies playing themselves audibly, visually before him, and as he stared at his future self, holding hands with her, he saw the future Aneurin – the happy Aneurin – shed a tear for him. *Why do you cry*, He asked: *I cry for pity*, came the reply, *because in a moment, I may cease to be.*

And Aneurin understood. It was like an abyss opened up before him: a limitless chasm which he must attempt to cross, for, shining, stood Aricie there, on the other side. They were friends, but would they ever be anything more?

'Ani?'

He snapped back to reality and realised he had been caught day-dreaming himself to a much happier place than now, a happier place of indecision, self-doubt and fear. She called through from the lounge.

'Did you hear a word of that?'

'Huh? Er...no...sorry, I was miles away.' He smiled sheepishly in what he hoped was an attractive way.

'I was just saying your answerphone is beeping at me.'

'Ok – thanks.'

He went back into the lounge, hit play and settled himself briefly on the sofa next to Aricie, perched on the edge to head back to the kitchen after the message had played. A woman's voice entered the cosy silence: she sounded in tears, and Aneurin had trouble placing who it was through the curtain of sobs.

'Ani? Are you there? Ani? Pick up...something terrible has happened...Oh Jupiter...it's your father...Ani, his plane crashed a few hours ago...they're looking but...so far...they haven't found anyone...Oh Jupiter...I...they think he's dead...'

She broke off into tears, and sobbed for a few seconds, and carried on, but Aneurin wasn't listening any more: he had frozen on the edge of the sofa, and Aricie had sat up straight next to him. Everything was numbed.

She was vaguely aware that the message had stopped playing.

The cosy silence devoured itself and became desolate.

The kettle finished boiling and clicked off.

He had been about to declare his love for the girl next to him, and now his father was dead. While a few seconds ago he had been torturing himself into self-destruction over an inadequacy, over his emotional psychosomacy, something that was really important – not just over-hyped inside his cranium, his idolisation, in his mind, so prone to excesses of miserable fantasy – something really important had happened, and his only reaction (he felt shame in it) was anger.

'Fuck!'

He shouted as he stood up, kicking the table over. He didn't even notice that Aricie's hand had been on his knee and now slipped uselessly by her side.

'For fuck's sake!' he screamed into the air.

He started pacing. She said nothing. It angered him. If she had spoken, it would have angered him too: the fact he'd kicked the coffee table over angered him, that he was angry made him angrier. He screamed again: at her, at himself, at his father, the gods, the injustice of it all.

'I brought you here to find out what happens if I tell you I love you, and instead we fucking find out my father is fucking dead!'

He realised what he had said. A part of him shrank in horror at opening his heart to so much potential pain. Then the rest of him thought at that small part of him: *that's nothing, there is so much pain flooding into your heart already...Dad...Dad's dead...*

She spoke quietly. 'Love me?'

He stopped his pacing. 'Yeah.' He threw it out almost as a challenge. *Love this, bitch.*

A few heartbeats fluttered.

'Ani...Ani, I... I love you too.'

Suddenly his anger cleared and his heart opened itself up to emotion. Tears began to trickle from the corners of his snow-white eyes, washing them brighter, cleaner, whiter. Grief hit him, and consumed him, and she reached out her hand, and he took it, and she cradled his head in her lap, and they sat there, hours, saying nothing, both in tears, him distraught, her hating to see him like this, crying, until the tears dried up in exhaustion, and they sat there, finding comfort in each other's presence.

Arrangements were made for them to fly back home, and it all passed in a daze. Before they knew it, they had arrived, Aneurin was descending the steps from the gleaming white plane to the black runway, hand in hand with Aricie. A rainbow was in his heart. He cried for his father. But the sun shone for Aricie. He had yet to meet Phèdre. And he felt guilt, and grief, and terror.

*

'And that's what happened. Please, don't tell anyone. I couldn't bear it...' Her voice trailed off.

'But, my queen, it was just a dream...sometimes these things just happen, and we overanalyse them. Damn our amateurish Freudian interpretations!' she scolded mildly.

'It was more than some id and ego fighting. This was something supernatural, more than a dream: The Oneiroi – all three! – were there. They were working some magic upon me.'

'Then it has nothing to do with you! It's not even anything in your mind, however overblown you could make it. Sometimes, it's just these damn gods rattling us...I'm sure that's all it is.'

Oenone looked like she had finished the conversation.

'I don't think so.'

Phèdre mused, more to herself. There was something that had been planted in her mind over this, a sickening realisation of truth that she had been trying to avoid. She thought that, like Freud had hypothesised, the Oneiroi only worked with what was inside the dreamer's mind – however deep it was buried.

'I think it means something. Something I haven't been willing to admit to myself.'

She had always felt, unconsciously, that she could lie to herself. It was a layer of self-defence within a layer of self-defence: she could lie to herself about lying to herself, and believe everything in its entirety. It was all so subconscious that she wasn't even aware of it specifically any more, just as a dull lifeless ache that filled her waking moments, and in torturous realities that penetrated her dreams.

'What do you mean? You never got on with Ani. You said so yourself, it's why he's in London, and you're here.'

'It's true. We never got on.'

The tone of her voice appeared convincing, but her lady-in-waiting knew her far better than that. She moved closer, and lay a hand on Phèdre's knee.

'What is it?'

Phèdre paced out onto the balcony, which looked out over the sea. Her room was on the topmost and westerly side of the palace, and it seemed like the sun was always streaming in. Her pale, weathered fingers gripped the railing as she leant over to look at the sea far below.

'Is it Aneurin?'

Silence always confirms too much.

'What about him?'

'Nothing, it's not to do with him.' She answered quickly.

Hurried speech always confirms too much, too.

'Jupiter, what is it?' Oenone breathed. 'He always seemed so nice – what is it he did, or is planning? Something against Theseus? We have to do something...stop it...whatever it is...I'll call – '

'No,' Phèdre interrupted, 'it's nothing like that. Do nothing.'

'Then what is it? You have been driving yourself to distraction ever since he left here, and you weren't exactly yourself since you met him either.'

Phèdre met the bland statement with silence. She moved back inside, out of the sun, and sat down, trying to control herself. She feigned interest in the pattern the window's shadow made on the floor, a delicate harmony of black and white on the monotone tiled floor.

She was beginning to get frustrated by this, and once again shame rose up inside her like so much bile overflowing from a scientist's beaker, surrounded by men in white coats making notes on the bile's texture, colour and quantity. She would be judged, for they were judging her. She couldn't be judged, there would be time enough for all of that, plenty of time in eternity…the anger began to boil at the injustice of it all.

'Isn't it fucking obvious?' she screamed at Oenone, who was taken aback at her sudden rage.

Some darkness had coloured Phèdre's eyes, Oenone saw, and that could only mean the presence of a powerful emotion. But was it love, or hate? There was a fine line between the two. She cast her mind back to decide which one: splintered memories raised themselves to her mind – sunshine and giggles on a picnic – deep intense discussions about boys – driving endless hours for a forgotten reason – family reunions / funerals – and Oenone realised with a shudder that came as a natural reflex that Phèdre's eyes had clouded with love.

Phèdre checked her temper. *Oh Jupiter* she thought, for she knew she had just given herself away. Oenone knew her too well not to know what had just happened. The macabre situation was unfolding, unravelling before her very eyes, and she knew that the gross secret she had harboured at the cost of her health for so many months was out, but instead of relief – a friend to share it with, a problem shared is a problem halved – she suffocated on her own guilt, for this problem shared was a problem quadrupled in value and increasing exponentially.

Every inch of her insides erupted upon themselves, devouring her with pain. She had been controlling her feelings for too long, forcing her darkest soul to unfold, pushing herself into self-destruction.

Phèdre immediately looked away, stared down at the floor, felt a tear leave her left eye and round the cheek before sliding down to the jaw, where it hung for a few seconds to admire its silvery wet trail, before it threw itself off her face into the abyss that separated it from the floor.

Her mind went blank yet filled with horror. Then she felt Oenone's fingers where the tear had committed its suicide jump, and her head was being moved up, and her eyes looked into

Oenone's, and saw – horror, as she had expected – but not hatred.

They were tinged with a sadness, a forgiveness, and a love she had not expected anyone to look upon her with once they knew her secret. For a second an understanding passed between them.

'Oh, Oenone,' Phèdre sighed, and embraced her tightly, as several silvery wet trails appeared on her cheeks, and more suicide jumps landed to their fate on Oenone's back. She felt accepted despite herself, and thought that even if she couldn't live with herself, the fact Oenone could live with her meant she could try to continue. She felt safe in her suite at the palace, and so everything span forth from her, and though each word was tinged with guilt, it was met without judgement, which – for Phèdre – was as close to happiness as she now thought possible.

'I first met him with Theseus, and I couldn't believe how alike they are. I saw him, and I blushed.'

She played down the nature of her reaction: she had not so much blushed as risked the explosion of her head as blood pounded upwards, reddening, suffocating.

'I feared to look into his eyes. If I saw Theseus, what I love in Theseus there, in him, then I may as well die on the spot. I avoided him as much as I could, made the polite answers, yearned to be with him, and away from him, and cursed the world…I burn!

'Now I pale to look at him: a tremble: a blur: my eyes no longer see, I can't speak. I was torn between freezing and burning all through, my fingers as icy as death and my heart as fiery as Hades. I knew that this was the work of someone beyond us.

'I fought it…fought it so hard…I built a shrine to her…burned incense all day long and intoned her name, asking forgiveness and for mercy.

'But I saw him everywhere – his face etched on clouds, in

trees, his memory stirred by a newspaper, a snatch of song, even the absence of anything to remind me of him still brought my ever-travelling mind back to him.

'Even on that happy day with Theseus, when we married, and I was determined to cast his son from my mind, just as we kissed to celebrate the union, my guilty eye caught *his*, and all the shame flushed upwards...I tried to cast him from my mind, but I keep hearing music playing in my head when I think of him.

'And worst of all...I kept seeing him in Theseus' face. Every time I saw my husband, I saw his son in him, and I loved him...every time we made love, every explosion, every joy, it wasn't Theseus there, but...'

She couldn't bring herself to utter his name.

'So I played the evil stepmother. I avoided him, and it wasn't hard to wheedle him away from this place. At least this thing had reminded me I was a woman, and I used that accordingly. It's not called manipulation for nothing.'

She emphasised the first syllable.

'I had him sent to study abroad. My passion abated when he was no longer there in front of me...my days were less troubled, the guilt lessened...but the nights...in the darkness, I tried to convince myself it was my husband I was with, rather than his son – but it was a hollow attempt to convince myself.

'I loved it in the darkness, for I knew that I could abate my guilt by pretending to believe that I believed the man underneath me was my husband and had nothing to do with his son: but instead I found that it was all the more sweeter for being unable to see him, because then I could fantasise that it was Aneurin, it was him, I was with him, and complete...even catching glimpses of Theseus in the moonlight could not shake my conviction, so alike are they...

'And it was amazing, but then in the sleepless nights after, the guilt flooded back...fought with passion over me...I fought them both, but the fiery passion is not mine but played out through me. Venus…'

'Venus!'

'Yes…it's to be expected really…mum…Ariadne…'

'You must forget. Until the end of time. Let an eternal silence hide that memory. Venus has no power over you – your husband is Champion of Greece!'

'Do not mention that!'

The sharp rebuke felt like an open fist hitting flesh.

'His power is irrelevant…Venus is awakening herself again. I fear the rest of my family is a precursor to me, I fear her rage will increase with every member of my line that walks this earth, or the world below.'

'But you are the last…'

'No, Oenone, I am not…a child grows in my belly…a future king…a future queen…a child…damned already.'

'You're pregnant?'

'Yes…but I…I can't keep her. It,' she corrected.

'Her?'

'If it's a girl…she's damned. Venus will make her burn. How can I bring a child into the world if her life is planned and damned? Better to save the child the trauma of existence…'

'An abortion? Phèdre…you cannot…it's murder…it's not your choice…'

'Not abortion…can't you see, Oenone? I am dying of guilt, and soon, I will be dead. All that is left is a prayer to Dad, and he will come for me, and this tortured affair will be over before tragedy has begun…it will only be me who suffers.'

'Only you? What about me? Others who know and love you?'

'I meant to take my secret to the grave…I never meant for you to become tainted.'

'That's not what I meant. I don't care about your guilt. But I can't watch you die.'

'Then leave now.'

'Phèdre! No! I love you too much for this…' She stared up at her face, but saw that she was determined, a granite look upon her visage. She knew argument was useless. But pleaded quietly, 'Phèdre…what comfort will death hold?'

Phèdre knew what she meant.

To stand before her father in hell and be judged. Looking back on her lifetime of torment, she realised that it would be unendurable torture to stand before him, have him look down upon her and dispassionately condemn her for her crimes.

She pictured the scene: just after the Ferryman, somewhere deep inside Hades, just at the entrance to the afterlife, she would stand on a pedestal and glow against the darkness, fire raging around her, as she pleaded to him for mercy.

But he would be cruel, would be cold: it was his job, and his nature, and he would have to be infinitely more cruel for his own blood. But what choice did she have?

If she stayed here, stayed alive, she would be standing before her grandfather on her mother's side, staring up at Helios, who gave so much light and warmth and life to the world, but for her shone down only darkness, and cold, and death. His gaze always blinded her. She felt herself shrivel up before him, and burn. The choice of pain between light and dark was equal, she could not stay living in the light, but nor could she bear to enter the darkness. The balance of pain hung unfettered, as it had her whole life.

But now there was something growing inside her that began to unsettle the balance: as it grew, it lent its weight to the balance, and began to tip into darkness. She loved her child, and the sacrifices one has to make for love are always incomprehensible, unthinkable, and ultimately unmakeable. Yet always have to be made.

She finally breathed a reply to Oenone. 'No comfort, for

me…but at least my child…she will not be damned…she will not face this choice…

'I die here, now, and take with me the last of my fated race, and Venus' power is broken. I'm sorry, Oenone…tell Theseus I love him…and say nothing to his son…'

She turned and spread her arms out, walking out to the balcony, displaying more energy than she had in months. She looked at the curiously energetic sea, and raised her melting eyes to the sky, and then closed them. Oenone crumpled heavily to the floor and started sobbing. Phèdre spoke in a clear voice into the bitter air:

'Hear me, Minos, Judge in Hades, and mine own father! My time has come. It is for me to choose, not you, and I ask you now to do my biding. It is time to die. Let me see you again.'

As she spoke, the air filled with crackling, and black lightning, and a cloud of pitch black appeared, wisping around haphazardly, teasingly.

'Father! Enough! Take me!'

The cloud shot out tendrils, and they felt their way towards Phèdre, who had a look of utter determination upon her face. They circled her, and then with sudden quickness, darted upon her stomach, and entered her.

The cloud disappeared, as did the tails of blackness into Phèdre. Her eyes opened in shock and she screamed in terror, and pain. She clutched her belly, and turned to face Oenone, who observed all the action with her gut rising.

'My child!'

Oenone felt she could see what was happening. A blackness spread over Phèdre's stomach, and she fancied she could glimpse a small foetus, with a dark heart, and a disfigured body, four heads, three toes, devouring itself, she could see the cursed smallness slowly start sucking life down the umbilical cord, which wrapped around one head, suffocating the halfling: the child was becoming a parasite, and was draining her mother.

Phèdre screamed in agony, and berated her father, 'How could you? Work through my child? She is innocent!' Another spasm of pain.

'Damn you!'

Phèdre was dying before Oenone's eyes, and Oenone knew she could not live without her mistress, and her best friend. Determined too, she searched the room with her eyes for a knife, or something she could grasp to slide into flesh and join her in her journey to Hades. There was nothing in sight, so she raised herself to her feet – such lethargy – and left the room, knowing she would find something soon to end this. Just as she reached the door, her hand stretching for its handle, it opened before her, and she thought she looked into a mirror: instead, it was Panopé, her eyes similarly filled with tears.

'Jupiter…it's Theseus…' She choked off.

'What is it, girl?' Oenone demanded.

'Theseus…he's dead.'

At these words, the black cloud re-appeared, and the tendrils of darkness left Phèdre and returned to their home. Oenone fancied she could see a grinning, mischievous face within the darkness, but it was gone before she could believe herself.

Phèdre slumped to the floor, and Oenone could see that her child was no longer a parasite within her. It was clear she had not heard Panopé's words, she looked confused, in disarray: it was up to Oenone to break this awful news.

She touched her on the shoulder, and those tearful eyes stared up into her own tearful eyes.

'Phèdre, Theseus…Theseus is dead.'

A sickening silence hung in the air, as all three women attempted to swallow the news. For two of them, the sickening silence felt like it entered them, for sickness consumed them. A wave of grief hit. Phèdre let out a primeval scream, but whether it was at the news of Theseus' death, or the failure of her plan, Oenone could not tell.

8

He had been travelling for days, and his feet were bleeding red. The rock he walked on was largely jagged and unaccommodating, it had not taken long for it to break through his shoes, and then his feet. He envied the Minotaur – at least he had a labyrinth to explore. His world here was an endless tunnel. He was not hungry, nor thirsty – something which mightily relieved him. He guessed wherever this place was, different rules applied – as he saw in the fantastical speed with which the river rushed past him – which meant despite his trekking for days he did not need food nor drink. He was relieved not because he had no food or water, but because of what he would have to do to get them: if he wanted to drink, he would have to enter the water, and he knew it would sweep him on and down into hell before he had tasted one mouthful.

Not that the river really classified as water: it was filled with black mud, dark writhing bodies and rotting corpses. If he wanted to eat, he would have to speak to call the creatures up from the depths, and then bash one to death with a lump of rock to eat from the putrid wreckage of his body. Neither method of sustenance appeared appealing, so he was grateful that he wasn't hungry or thirsty.

Was there a return from this place?

Although the obscure movement of time in this place meant he needed no refreshment, it did cause the journey to drag. He knew days had passed for him, and he slept when he was tired, and walked when he was not, but he knew back in the real world next to no time had passed.

It was an unsettling feeling, made more perversely unearthly by the music that floated down the river. At times inaudible, at others deafening, he listened all the time to music that made suicide seem a serious alternative (even with his hands over his ears he still heard it clearly.) It was strange that here, in this mystical place in between life and death, the only reality going was musical. It had no flaws: it soared and swooped, it dragged and dived, it was real and false, it was movement and stasis, and above all it was so invasively pervasive. He felt that the music was reality in this place.

Days slipped into weeks.

Brutal calluses developed to protect his feet.

He would speak to the dead, harrowing as it was, for the company.

It became tempting to end his journey, for so many days has passed – days beyond those he had counted, days in which he was not sure if he was hallucinating, or insane, and he knew he could reach his destination (wherever that may be) if he just jumped into the river and let himself be swept away in its muddy presence down to its end in a fantastic heartbeat of a second. He knew it would be suicide, but the music convinced him he didn't care.

There was something about the place that melded life and death in the sounds he heard, and it all made a beautiful sense. Yet he did not curtain his head beneath the muddy waves:

something held him back, and although it took him days of self-reflection to discover what it was, he realised it was his love for Phèdre, and Aneurin, and an ultimate desire to see his new son born, that stopped him entering the dark flowing liquid death.

Still he journeyed. He began to grow weary. The music began to grow louder, more coherent. He thought this might mean something, but death still seemed an appropriate alternative. The river began to narrow, but flow even slower: initially confused by this, Theseus soon realised that the river was deepening at an incredible rate. He tested his theory by calling to the dead: now only a few were close enough to the surface to haunt him. Soon, no-one answered his call.

As disturbing as they were, he felt himself miss the presence of others, even if they were more akin to demon than human. Eventually – dragging his feet slowly – Theseus passed through a narrow archway no wider than five metres, which opened up a space so large it may have been infinite. The river before him had become a lake, and the well of souls before him made him call out to see if the dead answered. He spoke in the tongue of Essil, which he had a feeling – from the music? – suddenly seemed appropriate.

Thus he spoke into the darkness (in subconscious but perfect timing with the music): 'Essil on, essil on erifet al.' †

He was astonished at what happened next. A voice answered, speaking in the dead tongue Essil, from the depths of blackness:

'Viðrar vel til loftárása, niðurlæging.' ††

He saw the speaker come gently into view: a cloaked figure, effortlessly propelling a small boat.

'I am Theseus, King of Greece and Champion of Neptune.' He bravely tossed the words to the incoming figure.

'Welcome Theseus, King of Greece, Champion of Neptune. I am the Ferryman. This is my world.' The boat glided to the shore and the man descended, appearing to float under his dark cloak, and stood before Theseus. 'Do not fear me.'

'Where am I?'

'The question is not so much a location of physicality, but a location of spirituality. This is the land between life and death, where the First Movement still plays untainted by neither life nor death. Here is the world as it was intended.' He spoke with an authoritative slowness.

'First Movement?'

The cloaked figure shrugged. 'So much has been lost to the ages. There was a time when the Champion of Neptune would have been aware of the First Movement.' He sighed. 'At least here you have time to be educated.' He gestured into the expanse. 'There is no time here. Sit.'

Obediently, Theseus sat. The figure sat down beside him, careful never to show his face from the folds of his cloak.

'The Champion of Neptune and his ilk have always had an affinity with the First Movement. It is born, I think, out of a desire for more once you are familiar with the gods, like an addiction. That is why your son calls on Apollo.'

'The gods are not the playthings of humans!' Theseus is suddenly angry that his son is on drugs: he knew the Ferryman's words to be true, because the mood the music created in him told him so.

'You have taken them on, and won.'

'That's different.'

'Why?'

'I'm the Champion of Neptune!'

'He will be too.'

'But not yet! He's messing with forces he cannot possibly comprehend. He couldn't take on the real powermongers...'

'Could you?'

'Yes.' Theseus answered defiantly.

The Ferryman let the sentiment hang there for a second.

'He is meddling with forces he does not understand, but he should look closer to home for things to fear. But let me get back to the First Movement.

'The world was created through song. There is a being beyond Jupiter, beyond Venus, Neptune, Vulcan, Helios, Minos – all the household names and powermongers. His presence is everywhere, but no-one knows of him anymore, and he has developed a martyrs complex. All music is an unconscious act of worship to him. Sometimes, he appears in music, especially if the listener has artificially heightened their awareness. He appears in many different guises – depending on what already exists in the listeners' mind. Like the gods you are familiar with, he develops what is already in your mind, which is just one more thing that they have stolen from him.

'All appreciation of music is a subconscious desire for him, for he is not love but an acceptance of being. He has created you with music in your soul, and your act of living creates a tapestry of noise that is beautiful to him. He created the gesamkunstwerk, the total art form, and we are all part of it.

'Let me show you.'

He reached out and touched Theseus' temple: suddenly the music around him came alive, and spoke to him. He realised how tired he was from his journey, and the thoughts became one with the music as they incorporated it into their song – was his mood defined by the music, or did the music define his mood? Music affects our state (e.g. minor music makes us sad) but does the gesamkunstwerk influence our emotions or do our emotions determine our interpretation of it? The music became flesh to him, and he spoke to it:

'Dry skin slides on snaky skin,
   Papery crack music plays,
    Haunts,
     Melody-less,

Infuses my being,
  Drives my inactive mind round till all spins,
   Till all is consumed,
    Physically crumpled,
     Pain is found in the comforting,
      Natural becomes a struggle,
       When the blessed blank noise comes to calm:
But it is the bass riff,
 The smooth bass,
  The riff of life,
   That permeates with precision,
    As the endless intro hums hypnotically so it spills
     Over, as the Saharan slits become damp once more,
      The subtle rhythms still stalk me as an endless and
       unwanted reminder.
Damn you!
Damn the music! Hail the mastery of the
 gesamkunstwerk!
   Bow to those who orchestrate it,
    Whose very presence is the ambience,
     The footsteps on the pavement,
      The inhalation,
       The exhalation,
The stem that links the rose-sweet petal heads to the living
 roots in the echoey cavern of my mind.
  The presence!
   The flawless artistry! The graceful ease!
 – But here I am, alone, with my bass rhythm.'

The Ferryman released his feather-light touch on Theseus, who breathed deeply, a slight tear in his eye. The song had taken three days to play.

'You have heard the First Movement for so long now that it has become a part of you. In this land, it is both life and death. It is everything in between. The being beyond it has no name, but instead the song is his title: the song that began before time and will continue after.

'He is the gesamkunstwerk, and to listen to it is so beautiful tears are never enough. There are so many reminders of him in the world that you live in, but you can never hear a pure gesamkunstwerk in your world, so you miss out on perfection.

'He exists in all sound, and in the absence of sound: if you enter a soundproof room, you will become aware of two things. First, a high pitched hum; and second, a low rumbling. The latter is the your heart beating. The first is your nervous system creating an electrical buzz. Music is forever. He is forever. His children live on: the Sirens are cruel, but were once his flesh and blood before they Fell, born of the union of music and woman.

'I live here in this world where the First Movement, that created the world, still plays. I am in perfect harmony with the song, just as the song is in perfect harmony with me, and it is my purpose to take the damned from one life to another. There is a path here that all must take: they enter through the Seal of Styx and are swept downstream in the river of the dead until they reach here, the Well of Souls. Here, souls that are ready, that have lost their fear, they surface, and I ferry them across the lake to Hades, and into hell, and before Minos himself.'

'Oh, great, the in-laws,' Theseus muttered to himself.

'This is the moment between life and death, or between death and the afterlife. The Well of Souls is death. The afterlife is life. They are all part of the same song, but the mind and in particular the soul has trouble letting go of reality. Many choose to stay out of hell in the lake: but they are driven mad by the promises the music makes to them, for in the infinite depths the sound is infinitely amplified.

'Most travellers come in the river, either birthing themselves into the afterlife at the Seal, or enjoying a perverse baptism as they give up on reaching the Well of Souls and hurl themselves, taunted by the First Movement, into the river. They certainly arrive in much less time than you, although of course time here is irrelevant.

'You are the first to make it here and converse with me without going through the purgatorial conflict of the Well of Souls. You are something of an anomaly, a peculiarity: your presence sparks a solo movement within the gesamkunstwerk, an unexpected harmony that adds a richness to the overall tapestry. Your presence sparks something tragic, but so tragically beautiful it has to be played out.'

'I understand,' Theseus breathed, the music making it make sense to him, 'there is something about tragic beauty, it is like finding violence beautiful but sad at the same time…'

He trailed off as the music once again assumed a voice that spoke to the pair, the Ferryman listening intently as if this was an unexpected development:

'Only two things in this world concern us: violence and beauty.

We want violence that's beautiful and beauty that's violent.

We want violence so beautiful that there is no pain, no blood, no fear.

Violence so beautiful there is no suffering and there is no anguish.

We want Man to realise the beauty in what he sees.

We want to find beauty in the way a cat sits on a fence at cold midnight.

We want to find beauty in the smile of an old lady passing you in the street.

We want to find beauty in the arrangement of glass and bricks (however broken).

We want to find beauty in muscle spasms, déjà vu and failed hindsight.

We want to find beauty not just in the eye of the beholder, but
in everyone's eyes.

We want to find beauty in the eyes of teachers, carpenters,
barmaids, drug addicts, alcoholics, soldiers, manic-
depressives, schizophrenics and suicidals.

We want to find beauty in the eyes of the sick, the angered, the
crippled, the hopeless and the depressed.

We need to see beauty in the coins of capitalism, in hangovers
and our oppressors' actions.

Although we are tired of plastics, vitamins and pre-packaged
foods; tired of rubber, chains and whips; tired of
sadomasochists and prison ships;

We long for harmony without strings and joy without pills;

And maybe, in a world where we can sleep without knives
under our pillows, maybe we can find, if we are sober
enough and strong enough to keep looking,

Maybe we can find beauty in the eyes of the sick, the angered,
the crippled, the hopeless and the depressed,

Perhaps there is a future in which we can see innocent beauty
in our children's eyes,

A future for rejected lovers to find more...'

The music emptied itself into another movement, and a new
voice sprang up, but Theseus could not hear it. The Ferryman
could, however, and it was a few minutes before he spoke again,
seemingly listening to the music for commands. Theseus spent
the few minutes wondering what the future held for rejected
lovers, and whether it was at all relevant to him. Finally, the
Ferryman spoke again.

'We are impressed with you, Champion of Neptune. You
travelled down the banks of the Styx before it is your time, and
we reward your perseverance. We also know that your part in
the solo movement is integral to the greatest beauty, the greatest

tragedy, the greatest harmony of the gesamkunstwerk, and accordingly, we send you back. The being beyond music is firing a warning shot at Jupiter and his motley crew, for he who once said "I am who I am" is now saying "I am who I am, and I am in charge."

'Farewell, Champion of Neptune: ág gaf ykkur von sem, varð að vonbrigðum. Petta er ágætis byrjun.' †††

With the parting words in the beautiful tongue of Essil still barely registering in his mind, Theseus found himself suddenly immersed in water, back on the Seal of Styx: true to his word, the Ferryman had sent him back, and he was already beginning to float off the metal. The water was calm. Time had passed, the storm had died, but Theseus did not know how long he had spent in the underworld, nor did he know how much time that was equivalent to in the overworld. He pushed off the seabed and swam upwards with powerful strokes to the surface: it was far away, but he made it without undue trouble. It was dark and he was tired. His journey had fatigued him, and he knew he was five miles from shore.

With a determined grimace, he started swimming.

He was discovered on the shore by an old French farmer out walking his dog near dawn. At first he thought he was a log (his eyesight no longer being what it once was) but his faithful companion soon roused his attention.

The man was middle-aged, he saw, but with a youthful face that was scarred by exhaustion and hypothermia. He dragged him to his nearby house, and put him to bed. He called a doctor who was sure he would recover, given enough rest. The man slept, unrecognised, for nine restless hours, before he awoke to a world that had changed beneath him while he walked down the banks of the river of the dead.

9

Panopé had left the room, leaving the two to grieve. Phèdre had moved to her bed, and Oenone sat next to her. The immediate pain had gone, although Phèdre thought if she moved, it could return. She lay perfectly still on the mattress, feeling herself sinking into it. Silence. What could be said?

Oenone took her cue from Phèdre, and sat beside her, stroking her hair occasionally. It was a futile gesture, like so much in life, but it gave Phèdre some comfort. She felt wanted, although she knew she could never be wanted, not with her guilt over Aneurin, and the sudden news of her husband's death.

A plane crash? She didn't understand. This was Theseus, Champion of Neptune. He had the protection of a god so powerful he intimidates heads of state with vast armies at their disposals. Neptune controlled the weather, and the water: the crash had taken place at sea, so surely Theseus had called upon Neptune to save him and his crew? How had he even allowed it to happen? Her mind baulked at the possibility that something beyond Neptune was involved: was it Jupiter? Why was he interfering? What plan of evil chaos was he trying to implement? And why was he inflicting such pain upon them?

Phèdre silently and inwardly cursed the gods. She had not the strength to curse them aloud and risk a showdown. She was as weak as the baby that grew inside her: perhaps weaker, for she could feel the child regaining its strength after Minos' ordeal, and the strength the child was feeding on was her own. She cursed her father, her grandfather, she cursed Venus: she cursed her mother, her sister; cursed Venus again, and Aneurin; she cursed Jupiter. She felt as if there was a vista of noise echoing around her, with a string section echoing cries of grief and a wailing voice intoning the end of the world and the crowning of misery and despair.

Her mind skipped. She had thought of Aneurin. What would she do about him? Even in this time of tumult, she burned for him. She felt sick at herself. She couldn't think things through straight: she needed another opinion. Although it had been hours that had passed since she had spoken to Oenone – hours that felt like lifetimes stacked up upon each other – she muttered the question into the physical silence:

'Aneurin?'

Oenone seized upon the possibility of a conversation. She had relegated the news of Theseus' death to the back of her mind as soon as possible as she cared only for Phèdre now, and desired that she could help her in this, the time of her grief. She had spent the past few hours thinking the situation through – it was an unusual one, all right, and one that required an unusual solution.

'I've been thinking…everything is going to be okay. Really,' she emphasised, as Phèdre scowled automatically. 'I've ceased urging you to live – I would have entered your grave with you. But this new sadness dictates different plans.

'Ani, without you, is nothing – a slave, an outcast, a bastard part of a rejected, discarded line. But with you, he could take his place as king.

'You must be there for him – who else will dry his tears? Who else can understand the tragedy that is unfolding? Who is more qualified than you?

'With you, he can be king. Theseus' death – I must appear cruel to say it, but I love you – has unchained your love. Your love becomes an ordinary love: the bonds that made a horror, a crime of your passion have been unforged, and you can see Aneurin guiltlessly.

'You are just two people, united in grief, sharing a destiny...you are already a family...just think...when you give birth, you can still be a family...' she swallowed hard, but it had to be said, it could happen, happiness sometimes works out for other people, 'perhaps a family with...you and Aneurin...together.'

At the mention of her baby, Phèdre moved her hand over her stomach. It was the first movement she had made in hours. Oenone had a point. Her love was no longer cursed: nothing tied her to Aneurin, except her passion, which flowed forth from her again. With Theseus dead, she needed a husband at her side, and a father for her child. Where better to find them than in the same blood?

It wouldn't be much of a change for her: for months now she had been living with Aneurin, not Theseus, making love to the younger, the elder being driven even further from her mind...and how she loved him...he would be her knight in shining armour, etched in brilliant white on the gloom of her first husband's death...some good would come from this...a smile spread across her face.

Take that, Venus...what you planned has been destroyed. My unholy passion has been rendered wholly acceptable...you have lost your battle against my race, and it was I, Phèdre, who *stopped you...*yes, this was a reason to live...there was hope...there was a family, there was love, and in the midst of such sorrow, happiness would grow, like a sapling fertilised by a rotting mulch of autumnally discarded leaves, growing, flowering, an ageless flower of jewelled beauty...

Oenone saw the smile flicker across Phèdre's face, and realised it had been so very long since she had last seen it. Indeed, Phèdre's face gave a convoluted twitch as the muscles spasmed in an unfamiliar fashion: for a second, Oenone thought she saw another face smile in the spasm of muscles, but it must have been her imagination, because Phèdre was radiant now, although she looked pale against the black sheets.

Oenone looked down on the smiling Phèdre and knew she had communicated with her, that her message, and all its connotations, had got through. And from the smile on her face, she was determined to follow her advice. Phèdre would declare her love for Aneurin in this time of grief, and they would be drawn together, and the love would be reciprocal, and circular, and they would raise the child, born outside the power of Venus' watchful gaze, and they would have children of their own, and everything would be perfect, because Phèdre loved Aneurin, and Aneurin loved Phèdre.

*

As expected, there was a message asking for Aneurin to go straight to Phèdre upon arrival. He crossed the dark tarmac and made to enter the gleaming white state car, when he turned, and looked back at Aricie. He was being hustled away, and she mouthed at him across the growing divide *it's okay.* She appreciated this was a family thing, she would follow, and be there for him when he needed her.

Damn it, no, he thought. He wasn't leaving her like this, being swept off in his officialdom by bustling people with broad shoulders and black jackets and earpieces. He strode back towards Aricie.

'Come with me.'

'I can't. Ani – this is a family thing. Grief. You and Phèdre share a bond now...go be with her...I know your fears, but maybe you'll help. She'll still appreciate it.'

'But I want you there with me.'

'I know. But don't worry. I'll follow...ring when you get a chance...I'll call to let you know where I am.'

'Okay.' He took her hand, and gave her a peck on the cheek. Despite the flight and the sleepless night, her skin was soft to the touch, and she smelled fragrant and beautiful.

'I'll call you soon.'

And he headed back to the car, got in and was driven up to the palace, through the acres of coastline to the cliff-top palace, up to see Phèdre. He passed the stables and the spit where he trained Pegasus and Tristar, remembering his childhood working with them, playing with them, training endlessly in bright hot sunshine. He had such a gift with them that he could talk them into traversing the razor-sharp rocks that separated the sandy beach from the dusty land.

The palace came into view, suddenly, cinematically. It was constructed from dark jade, and white chalk, and the whole structure was a monochromatic mess, imposing yet ineffectual. It seemed to stagger, spreading itself out haphazardly: balconies hung themselves over the sea, seemingly unattached to the architecture. His room had a particularly fantastic balcony, although it was tucked cosily away on the first floor, didn't look out over the sea, and wasn't nearly as impressive as the one in the Queen's suite.

An impressive pseudo-Gothic building, the palace pre-dated Gothicism by hundreds of years, having been built by the gods themselves in a declaration of their independence from the Vault. Although Aneurin had said the Vault was in the grounds of the palace, perhaps it was more accurate to say that the palace was in the grounds of the Vault. He had been shown it once by Theseus, but had been forbidden to enter. He hadn't really wanted to, either, as there was something deeply disturbing in the atmosphere of the place.

He cast the unease from his mind. He remembered that afternoon when Theseus took him to the Vault: a good day. He missed him. But his mind wasn't focused on Theseus; nor was it focused on his meeting with Phèdre, which worried him.

What occupied his thoughts on the journey was Aricie, and the fact he hadn't kissed her yet, and he felt a surge of guilt about thinking about this so soon after his father's death, for they hadn't even found the body and started the purification and burial rights. He hadn't met Phèdre.

And yet – his mind was – still – on Aricie.

10

Phèdre was waiting for him in her suite, sitting with her back to the entrance, looking out at the sunlight that streamed through the glass doors that opened onto the balcony. The sea glinted through the glass. He could only see her arm on the side of the chair, but he noticed it looked pale, as if she hadn't seen natural light for months. Her lady-in-waiting, Oenone, was lurking silently in a corner, avoiding them both. Figures, he thought, this is a family time. He came up quietly to her.

'Phèdre…I'm so sorry…how are you?'

She heard his words and rose to meet him. Yes, she was pale, and thin too. But she seemed to draw strength from the sunlight. Her heart fluttered slightly, childishly, at the sight of him.

'Ani,' she breathed, and leaned forward to embrace him. She felt her movements were so clumsy and there was an age of eons as she leaned into him, and for a second she almost became confused, and could not remember why she was leaning into him – was she approaching for a kiss? – but then she wrapped her arms around him, and held him to her tightly.

*I see my husband here, before my eyes, I see him, my heart...I'm lost...this frenzy, passion, bursts in spite of me...*She let out a soft sob, and a tear trickled down her cheek. Oenone saw the trickle and understood her agony: declaring love is the hardest task one can attempt, and so very rarely complete. But she had hope for Phèdre.

'Don't cry,' Aneurin said as he heard Phèdre sniffle, 'I'm here. Together, we can get through this.'

He wasn't sure what he should say – what could he say? – there are never the right words to comfort grievers. Actions always mean more: a supportive hug, the right glance passing between you, the unspoken connection...all of which were missing from the awkward embrace. They broke away from each other.

'You look well...it has been so long since I've seen you...you look well...and so much...' she hesitated, 'so much...like your father.'

He did not know what to say. Words deserted him as his mind spun, but the barrier between language and communication reared its ugly self into the conversation, as he found himself unable to articulate the myriad of emotions and thoughts that jostled for position within his tortured cranium. He sort of stuttered a mumbled nothingness in reply.

He took that compliment well. Now to continue this. She surged with a thrill of confidence that was not her own.

'I am sorry we do not meet again under happier circumstances...I do not understand it, and I grieve for it. Theseus, my husband, and your father, is gone from us. But though he is gone, I still see him here...in you...he will live on...in us...'

She had rehearsed this speech so many times in such a short space of time that she thought it was both so undeniably beautiful he would have to fall for her and so clearly argued there could be no other possibilities of thought. But as she started her speech, things immediately began to diverge from her rehearsed possibilities: tiny things assumed significant proportions as her conscious mind concentrated on them (her emotions: the weight of her clothes: how large her feet suddenly seemed) while her unconscious mind speeled through her speech. She had never rehearsed to Aneurin's face either, and though she thought she had predicted his response, his face spoke volumes to her about his internal distress and confusion. She paused for a moment.

'Yes, he will live on in us, in you and me.' Again a pause. Surely he would speak this time.

'I mourn his passing…damn it, I miss him already. It's so sudden, y'know?' His casual honesty sparked something inside her. 'But he won't live on in us. He's dead. We have our memories of him, memories of all the times we will cherish. And that's what we have to stick hold of, to be true to. We will never forget him, but that's not the same as him living on, is it?'

He wondered why she was holding on to the trite platitude of the dead remaining with the living. It was only true if you lived inside your skull, living with your memories, but spending too much time in there would drive you into depression.

She blushed to hear him speak like that. *I didn't expect him to say that…never in my dreams, wishes, visions did he react like this...what next?* She surged with lust as she started her next sentence, but by the time she finished it, the lust had faded and was replaced with self-loathing. Where had that unexpected burst of emotion come from?

'It's not the same…but we have the next best thing. You are his own blood. I am…was…his own wife. And…and I carry his own blood too.'

She had planned all these conversations like a flowchart, mapping out the possible replies and then planning answers that all led to the central crux that they were here to discuss. His reply had been unexpected, but she had managed to salvage the situation. She had leapt forward through several chapters of her planned dialogue – missing the explanations of her longings, the subtle flirting, the recalling of dreams, the slow and steady build to her announcement of a child, and then onto her declaration – and she had just announced her pregnancy to Aneurin.

He was immediately aware of the ramifications. Primogeniture law was unclear in a situation such as this: technically, Phèdre would rule until her child was of age, while Aneurin was now an outcast, part of a defunct family line, fit only to inherit a tribe now lost deep in Amazonia. He was immediately worried, despite himself. She saw this worry etch itself on his face.

'You're pregnant?'

'Yes, but do not worry, prince…as I said, Theseus lives on in us…and I mean *us*. You and I. I carry his blood…you are his blood…together, he can barely be missed, except in our hearts, and – with time – maybe then the pain will go, replaced by the "us" that we will become.'

'Dear god, what do I hear? Do you forget that Theseus is my father? You're his wife?' *What is she saying?*

'What makes you think I've forgotten that?' *Why is he reacting so?*

'Forgive me.' He blushed. *How disgusting…how could I think that? Such a misinterpretation brings shame upon me…how can she ever forgive me thinking that of her? Dad…*he felt ill for a second…*Dad would be disgusted…*

'You spoke in innocence. I'm sure I misinterpreted your words. I'm so ashamed…I cannot look…I'll go…'

He turned to leave. A thrill of foreboding poured through

Phèdre as she felt something flow from outside her body, through it, and exit again: she felt as if everything had gone to plan, at least to her hastily readjusted plan, and everything was at the final moment when it would all slot into place. This is the moment people would be talking about for years, how two lives torn asunder in terror would be united through grief and by love. She grabbed his arm and pulled him around. Again, she wasn't sure if she was going to kiss him, but she used her lips differently, and spoke definitely, defiantly to him:

'Don't be so cruel: you understood me all too well. You shall know me: I love you. Take your place at my side, upon the throne, and we will rebuild this happy empire and this happy family.'

She was caught up in the sudden thrill of the outpouring of her emotions, and she felt herself getting carried away, but not by her own buoyant emotions – no, by something else, just outside reach, and just outside comprehension –

'Stand by me, us together, and assume your place at the head of the throne and the head of this family. Be a father to this child, and we will smite Venus, for she can have no power amongst us. Let us smite her! Us, together Ani, can you not see it? Open your eyes to the possibilities that result, to all the potentialities that have become ours, to the perfections that spiral into existence at our every moment of choice…oh Ani, now you see this, you can know me in my entirety: I love you.'

The last few words were audible. But choked in Phèdre's throat.

What she had told him had made the world fall away. He seemed to back off from himself through a small rectangular hole in the back of his skull until he felt floaty light looking down on his body: it was almost like being out of his own body, but still very much in control. The distance between his consciousness and his body made it hard for him to control his body, like operating a machine from a distance, so you overstretch, and small movements become magnified as you shake.

He was in shock, and a numbing movement ended with strings uttering out a sweeping melancholy of dramatic potential.

'Phèdre, I…' he started.

His eyes must have betrayed him. A pain began to grow across her face. She started too, 'Aneurin, I…'

Both sentences choked in their throats.

Aneurin felt as if you would feel if you had all the time with the brazen soundtrack haunting you in your ear. As if you had entered some empty labyrinth:

The corridor, travelling downwards, in murky black, you feel yourself tending towards depression, but finding your feet (as fleet as thoughts) keep taking you there until you realise that you have arrived and cannot unarrive. Worse, you realise where your thought-feet have taken you is no different from where you started: you are merely circling around the same issue, passing from room to room in this labyrinth of self-pity and despair.

Always the broken strings taunting.

Glance about your journey: check for a horizon, or just an end to this infernal eternal corridor, anything to break the monotony of sealed door after sealed door. The numbers on the doors (assuming they are numbers; but you do see a pattern) are in some foreign tongue, alien markings that may be the way out but rely too much on fluid intelligence, with a perceptive reading of your environment and the body language of others, for you to be able to comprehend what the gouged script says.

A drone mocks you in its attempt to alleviate passion.

You used to check if the doors were open; but then you

figured you would get to the end quicker if you didn't check every door. That was three years ago, and now you've just given up on doors, and walking, and love.

A stirring bass line moves down the corridor. You do not hear it, but instead feel the air particles moving. Are you deaf?

You utter a few words: but astonished to find only barbaric grumbles, you put your hand in your mouth – and find no tongue. How did I speak? you think. How long have I been without my tongue? You are mute in this world that has been constructed for you. You cannot find a way out. There is a muscular stump waving in your mouth; with a sickening retch, you realise it is what remains of your tongue, and you are screaming.

Phèdre felt shame rising from her pallid empty stomach, almost tasting the dimness of her bile. She swum with a thousand dark-eyed angels as they took her, cajoling and harassing her, downwards and darkwards:

You see these non-corporeal beings dressed in murky robes, and you hear them whispering to you, subtle and endless reminders of a passion that is unearthly in its conception and its construction.

You remember the night when the sun set and demons crawled in / And whispered spite into skulls, tales of / Evil dementure and satanic eruptions of / Anger. Self-destruction. / Eyes reflect the apple as their irises / Show death, desire for death, hopelessness.

You see hopeless pupils, stare blankly forwards, you can feel them, feel them take control. They have scared you, scared you absolute.

You feel them, feel them take control. Angels with darkened eyes grip you with strangely cold hands, veins raised and a grip of calloused strength. What do they whisper to you?

You strain to listen, but their voices utter a foreign tongue. They gesticulate wildly at you in the hope that comprehension will dawn, but your mind is flooded by the sheer number of dark eyes that smother you.

You see a glint of happiness, or something close to happiness, in their eyes as you sink down in the blackened river.

You realise that this glint of happiness only occurs when you make progression into the depths. With a tired sigh, muttered slightly under your breath, you give yourself up to the dark currents and the dark-eyed angels, and sink further into the black sea of shame.

The silence just hung there.

Phèdre's eyes searched for Aneurin's. His eyes were not his own, and an unfocused gaze stared down at the floor past Phèdre. Through no conscious effort, his eyes avoided hers. He didn't even notice hers striving for his. Hers flicked left and right, searching for an opening into his, a small chink in his stunned armour.

The silence just hung there.

Her searching eyes looked at him. She was sure she hadn't breathed since her words choked in her throat, and she was sure that that was eighty-seven thousand, eight hundred and forty seconds ago. Finally, there was movement.

He raised his head, and her lungs allowed air in again.

He looked up at her. His eyes regained some focus, and her lungs allowed air back out.

Then he closed his eyes. And her soul froze.

Suddenly the silence was broken by a strangled gasp from Phèdre: the sound of drowning hopes and swimming fears coming into her reality. She turned and fled from him, Aneurin's closed eyes blocked her fleeing visage from him, and he did not see her heartbreak etched across her face, did not see the tears trickling down, did not see the storm clouds of despair blacken the room. He heard two sets of clattering footsteps – Oenone, a witness to the scene, left with Phèdre – the footsteps make their way outside, a dull echo serving as a fading reminder of what had just occurred. He heard sniffles. All this his ears heard, but his mind did not register. It had just shut down.

The horror, the horror.

He sank to his knees. A tear trickled down his own cheek. What had just happened? How did this happen? What was going to happen now? He opened his eyes. Phèdre was gone. The room appeared cavernous, its extremities cloaked in a muddy murk. A darkness seemed to fall. He tried to force his mind to process what this meant: his stepmother had just declared her love for him on the very day his father died.

Unholy declaration.

Immorality made flesh.

Passionate rejection.

He felt his stomach retch and fought the rising tide with peristalsis. But the liquid that was in his stomach slipped through the contracting muscles, and Aneurin felt his mouth flood with discoloured acid, which he released from himself with a mightily relieved spasm. If only he could eject the contents of his mind along with his stomach.

Self-loathing and horror flooded up around him as he descended, led dancing by a half-man half-beast, into the realms of self-pity. This was unliveable. He had no idea what to do. Who could he turn to, to collapse in an insensate heap? To watch him as rivers of salty tears swept his emotions away?

He felt a vibration in his pocket. Automatically, more by habit than force of mind, he slipped his mobile from his pocket. He forced his eyes to focus on the glowing screen, but it was a while before the script became legible. Six letters accompanied the trite icon of a phone ringing: six letters that suddenly meant everything to him. Six letters that spelled out the only place he wanted to be, the only place he could find himself in at a time like this, a place where he could be an insensate heap of salt rivers. Six letters.

Aricie.

He pressed the answer button, and held the phone to his ear.

'Aricie?…Sweet Venus…' he started, surprised to find his voice wavering. 'You'll never believe this…'

'Ani, listen to me,' she interrupted seriously. Something in her tone made him stop. 'It's your dad…' An insensitive pause followed.

'What about him?'

'He's…well, he's…Ani, sit down. He's alive.'

'Alive?'

'He survived the crash. Something strange happened. He's on his way back now – all he can think about is getting back to his family.'

Something about that word lurched sick on Aneurin's mind, and again he felt his stomach rise. This time, he kept the putridity inside with a grimace. The news of his father had lined his stomach with lead. Aricie continued unaware, 'We're not sure what's happened yet, but we think he's uninjured. Where are you? He's coming back on the royal helicopter, he'll be landing at the palace. Where are you?'

'Oh, Aricie…something terrible has happened.'

'What is it? Phèdre?'

'Phèdre! Does she know about Dad?'

'I don't know…only a few of us were there to hear…I called you straight away. Someone may have told her. Why?'

'Fucking Jupiter! Aricie, we have a problem. Where are you? I need to meet you.'

'I'm in your room. You sound terrible. I'll be here waiting for you.'

11

Theseus awoke in a musty-smelling room, covers pulled up tightly about him. He ached all over, and was consumed with tiredness. His eyes refused to open, and as he reached to rub them into openness, he felt thick skin caked onto his fingertips. Suddenly the bizarreness of the situation returned to him: he had travelled down the Styx for months, met a peculiar being who spoke to him truth about music, and then returned him back to a timeless present…he remembered little after that, except that he had a long way to swim, and he was so tired…

He sat up. He must have been rescued by someone. Did they know who he was? Probably not, if he was still sleeping here. What time was it? What day was it? He looked at the clock, and the calendar beside his bed: the calendar said three months ago: it had obviously not been changed since then. Was it in French? He groaned. It was late in the evening. He had to get up, meet his hosts, thank them, phone home, and get the hell out of here.

He was too close to his memories of that place where time had stood still, and he was beginning to feel ill because the gesamkunstwerk no longer played audibly to him. As an illness engulfed him, however, he thought he felt the music alongside him; felt, not heard. Perhaps it became easier to hear in moments of heightened emotion or physical distress? As his mind attacked this possibility, he was distracted from his illness, and he felt the music slip away. Definitely possible.

He swung his legs over the side of the bed. His feet were still blackened: even his swim to shore had not washed clean his dark instruments of movement. They hurt too. He had to get himself properly sorted out, and get himself home.

Home: where his family were. For the first time in months, something settled within him: there was no wariness, no anguish, no unease. He was thinking about his family: yes, a return home, to see Phèdre (how he had missed her, longed to be with her, to smell her and feel her next to him) and then he would take her to London, they would go and visit Aneurin, stay there for a few days, a week or two, spend time with each other, he could see his son being the man he had become. He itched to get home.

The door opened, and a French farmer's head came around the corner. Theseus smiled and waved hello, cursing his lack of attention in French classes. He mimed a telephone sign at the farmer, who nodded comprehension and beckoned Theseus to follow him. The pyjama-clad king followed mutely.

*

I am alone in this room. It is dark. I never wish to see anyone again, because if I do, it means that they are looking upon me just as I am looking upon them. And if they are looking upon me, then they are seeing all the shame and guilt rise like bile within my breast, and they are watching me in my agonies as they judge me.

I will keep this room dark forever because there is nothing to be held for me in light: my dazzling founder stares down upon me, and I can feel my skin shrivel and burn before his gaze. It's all his fault anyway. Why did he have to reveal anything to Vulcan? The affair was so secret, so quiet, wasn't hurting anyone, but still he chose to reveal Venus' secret, and the repercussions are so intense, so vast, that they are still being felt...

Damn you Venus! You make me burn, and I am the first to be abhorred by my own passion, by your passion that you put in my heart and make me play out for your own petty amusement....

And the sudden memory of events...makes my heart shudder...as I remember how Aneurin rejected my being, my self, my very existence, how in his refusal to acknowledge me, to close his eyes upon me, to shut the windows of his soul fast upon me, how his actions cut my existence into worthlessness as I know I can never love again how I loved Aneurin, and now the emptiness of reality springs up around me as sobs burst forth from myself although I try to remain composed, and damn you Venus!

It is your fire that burns in me, and despite all my attempts to placate you (I have burned incense at your altar and intoned your name) you still wish to punish me although I have done nothing to you! Did you have all this planned before I was born? I am innocent, was born in a state of innocence, and would have remained there if you had not interfered, and you did, you brazen hussy, you have tainted my family line, and I am just another – oh the sympathies with Mum and Ariadne, how they come flooding around me, this passion that bursts forth in spite of ourselves, and how could Aneurin reject me so? I am dead now: my spleen leaks itself into my bloodstream, and I can feel what I have become take over me as I start to die again, but this a natural death of jilted rejection...

what's wrong with me

all those happy possibilities GONE
they were almost memories
from the future
a future that will never happen
because my rejection is so complete

A bright light suddenly enters the room, and I shrink from it as it seeks to burn and judge me: I see a door has opened, and a figure is entering – no, go away, whoever you are, I must be alone – but it is Oenone, and she is the only person who does not judge me, for she has a beauty in her soul that prevents her from wishing death upon me, which is what everyone who knows me must do in order to save themselves, what is this, Oenone is entering, and she is speaking to me, can I understand her words, yes, she is saying something, and I hear her, and understand, and I do not know what to do, I am not sure who it is that I love, and I do not know what can be said, what will be done, but I know we must all meet, and I fear that this could be the end of everything, for if this dark secret was to come out, it would be the end of everything, for if Aneurin tells, then yes, I will have to kill myself rather than stand in this world again, and I will not rely on Minos again, and I shrivel in a corner in darkness as Oenone speaks her words to me, and I understand them, and my world explodes even further into tragedy.

*

Oenone enters the room, and her eyes cannot adjust to the gloom, but she hears a scuffle as a figure moves out of the light and backs into a dark corner. She knows she has found Phèdre. She recounts her news, the terrible unfolding of the truth, but there is no response from Phèdre. She squats down, and looks at Phèdre: her eyes have adjusted now, and she can see her visage in all its tortured glory. She repeats her news.

'My queen? Did you hear me? … Theseus is alive…he is on

his way back here now…'

Now that Oenone can see Phèdre's face, she can see that Phèdre has heard and understood the news. The terrible tragedy of the situation unfolds, and Oenone can read it on Phèdre's face: she does not know what she is going to do, but she is ready to take the ultimate step again, and wish death on herself, and she is so determined that if death cannot be wished upon herself, then it will be visited on herself by her own hand…

This was something that Oenone could not allow. She had to save Phèdre, mainly from herself. She had to put her mistress beyond doubt and above suspicion, put her – despite anything that Aneurin might say – completely in the clear. She loves Phèdre, so she must blacken Aneurin before his father. A sudden plan formed in her, and she felt she could hear music playing somewhere, miserably. She had to destroy Aneurin's reputation to save Phèdre, but what is a reputation compared to a human life? Aneurin would live somewhere else, banished, and Phèdre would live here, and come to love Theseus again. Yes. She was doing the right thing.

*

'I have become a horror to myself.'

Aneurin and Aricie were together in his quarters: his room had a fresh cleanliness to it, but the peace and tranquil quiet of the room was disrupted by their presence: a darkness of mess spun out from their crumpled bodies lying next to each other on the bed, spreading out into the sterility.

'What are you going to do?'

'What can I do?'

'Tell Theseus?'

A pause.

'I cannot.'

'Why?'

'It would kill him, destroy him, break him entirely. He loves Phèdre so completely. He also loves me completely. To hear this would destroy him.'

'So you aren't going to say anything to him? What about Phèdre?'

'I don't think she'll be telling him anything soon. She probably wants to forget all this. I know I do.'

'Just pretend it never happened?'

'I guess…though how can I? She has made me a horror to myself. I think of her with sorrow, compassion and fear. I feel sorry for Theseus, who is caught innocently in the middle. Yet what can I do? I must hold my silence.'

Quietly: 'I think you should tell him.'

Aneurin stood up and walked away.

'I cannot. I will not. And I must ask you to say nothing too…there are times when there is no place for the truth. Whatever is said, I ask you, I beg of you, to hold your tongue and keep your silence. I have trusted you, and I ask you keep my confidence.'

Aricie stood up and walked over to meet Aneurin. She took his hand, and looked him straight in the eye, and with the eye contact, everything became assured, and Aneurin suddenly felt all his self-disgust drain away from him. He was reborn as himself, reborn in innocence in Aricie's gaze.

'I don't understand fully, but I will keep my silence, because it is what you want.'

Aneurin breathed a sigh of relief, and smiled. Aricie smile back, again that jewelled look of seductive beauty scattering itself across her charmed features. And then. She moves closer. And closer still. He has never been this close to her. He looks deep into her eyes and sees only himself there. Then her eyes close slowly, and she tilts her head. A thrill of anticipation runs through him. She rises up, and he leans down. And then. Their lips meet. And then. They meet again. And then. He closes his eyes, and takes her into his arms, and her hands are running over the back of his head, and he pulls her in tight to him, and feels her body move against his, and her tongue snakes into the corner of his mouth, as his dances on hers, as they clinch and then break apart for breath and then go back again, tilting their heads the other way and exploring the opposite corners of each other's mouths as the intimate moment passed between them. A piano score echoed slightly in their ears: floating and effervescent. He opened his eyes, and stared at her so close there right in front of him, everything was so magnified up close, and he looked at her eyelids, and even though he could not see her eyes (those gladed pools of perfection) he found something intensely beautiful about her eyelids and the look of passionate concentration on her face, and he closed his eyes, and leaned into her again, and continued to kiss her. The piano score echoed perfection.

'Good night,' she whispered, and slid to one side of the bed, a smile on her face, turning her back on him and ending the evening.

12

The king was due to arrive back at any moment along with the dawn: palace servants had scuttled away to gather the relatives ready to receive him. They found Phèdre tucked away in a room in her quarters with the curtains closed, tear streaming down her face, allowing only Oenone close to her. She had not slept. With some persuasion they convinced her to go down to the entrance hall to meet the returning king.

Aneurin had not slept either. He was enraptured by his own thoughts, spinning endlessly as he lay restlessly besides Aricie. She slept soundly, but he drops in and out of an uncomfortable insomnia. It was only as she turned over in her sleep that Aneurin felt calm – she looked so peaceful as her delicate features rose and fell to the tune of her perfumed breath. For a second, and then another, and on in to the lengthy night, time froze as he found comfort in her perfection. He watched as she gradually became brighter as dawn illuminated the room, and slipped out before someone came to wake them.

He knew he would have to face Phèdre, and the returning king.

For both Aneurin and Phèdre, as they moved to meet the king, their feet felt encased in lead as they descended the marble staircase into the impressive hallway. Its cavernous ceiling swirled with a black and white pattern, and the steps alternated between the monochromatic colour scheme that spread itself around the palace.

Every step was an effort, as if they were walking through fluidic air, and they had to forcibly make way for their moving limbs, their turned heads, and their downcast eyelids.

She saw him first. He was making his own way down one staircase on the other side of the hallway. Even as she stood in the hall watching him walk down the staircase, as she stood awaiting her husband's return from the grave, she stood there and indulged a sexual fantasy…her eyes misted over, but then through the haze of day dreaming fantasies it registered that he had seen her, and she shook her head clear and turned away. Where she had just coursed with lust, self-loathing now filled her.

He saw her standing at the bottom of the opposite staircase, and his stomach gave a lurch that seemed to ripple through his entire body. He missed Aricie: if she had been there, she would have squeezed his hand encouragingly. He thought back at her lying peacefully asleep, and knew where he wanted to be. He pulsed with a sudden energy and strength of will, and took a deep breath, and – feeling renewed, and ready – carried on down the steps, one at a time, then another, left foot, right foot, all so careful and deliberate, until then, finally, he stood at the bottom of the hallway, and opposite Phèdre.

The silence was palpable. He thought: *last time I saw her, she said she loved me, and wanted me to be the father of her children.* His mind ached with disdain and illness.

The silence remained. She thought: *last time I saw him, I still had hope that we could be together, us, perfection combined.* Her mind filled simultaneously with lust and self-disgust.

And still there was silence. It was awful: the bustling minions noticed how everything was awkward, but did not say anything. Only the individuals at the centre of the hallway comprehended the scene in its entirety, and both camps were uncomfortably ill at ease in the other's company. Eye contact was avoided at all costs.

Finally the great doors to the hallway opened with a bang that shattered the silence and snapped the tortured duo to attention, and in strode Theseus, a huge grin on his face and his arms outstretched.

'Phèdre! Ani! So good to see you!'

He practically ran up to them, and Aneurin was slightly closer to him, so he swept him into his arms. There was something muted in the hug he received back though, but he dismissed the thought from his mind as his arms encircled his child, and his heart swelled with love, and he felt like he was home. The embrace lasted for a time, but then the happiness was cut with the gasp of barely controlled tears.

Theseus turned to see his wife, expecting her to launch herself into a passionate embrace. Instead he turned round to see her clutching her hand to her mouth, looking in incomprehension between himself and his son, eyes unfocusing themselves, and stifled tears gasping their way from her eyelids. He stepped forward to embrace her, and comfort her, but he saw her take a sharp step backwards, almost stumbling on her dress. He went to open his mouth to tell her *it's okay, I'm fine, it's me, I'm back home* but she spoke too quickly for him, and he could not tell whom she was addressing.

'You have been greatly wronged!' And she tearfully turned and fled.

Happiness turned to confusion on Theseus' face.

The sound of Phèdre's footsteps echoed away as he turned back.

Aneurin turned his eyes desperately away.

'What the hell is going on?' He demanded angrily. 'What is this all about? Who has been greatly wronged? Me or you?'

Aneurin answered as truthfully as he could,

'We both have. Maybe we all have.'

The answer did nothing to placate his father, and as Aneurin saw the anger rise up inside Theseus, he knew the truth was the only thing to say in this situation, and he knew he could not say it, and there was only one thing left for him to do, so he turned, and fled. Theseus did not stop him going: instead, he turned a full circle in complete bewilderment, looking to someone, anyone, for answers – but the hallway that had been so full so recently was now devoid of bustling staff, all fearful of what was being played out in the theatre-like entranceway. He spoke out angrily into the emptiness.

'Will someone tell me what the hell is going on?' His voice echoed slightly, and he heard a scuffle in the corner, by the doorway Phèdre had fled from.

'You! Oenone! Halt!'

The figure tremulously obeyed.

'Come here!'

She breathlessly approached.

'Tell me what the hell is going on here before I *really* start to lose my temper!'_

She spoke fitfully, fearfully, nervously: he assumed she was terrified of his righteous anger, but in reality, she was terrified of what she was about to do. The same cold, calculating logic that had persuaded Phèdre to announce her suddenly-pure love to Aneurin again surfaced to the melting pot of emotions that simmered within Oenone, and the solution to this disastrous mess appeared clear as daylight and just as shimmering, just as dangerous. But this had to be a superb act, she thought, and started hesitantly.

'I...er...no...I must see to Phèdre. She needs me.'

'You are not leaving until you tell me what is going on! Now speak, and be done.'

'I...I cannot.'

'Oenone, unless you tell me what happened, I will banish you from my kingdom and you shall never see Phèdre again. *Tell me what has happened.* Who has been greatly wronged? And how?'

'...it is you...you have been greatly wronged.'

His worst fears were confirmed.

'How?'

He was met with silence. He grabbed her by the arms and looked her straight in the eyes, shaking her slightly. '*How?*'

'It's Ani...and Phèdre...'

His stomach lurched. He'd always suspected they never entirely liked each other, but they'd always been civil, hadn't they? What had happened while he was away? If it had been an argument, this was all blown out of proportion...he'd calm everything down, get them talking again, it would all be smoothed over, just fine...

'What about them?'

'I die to say it...but your son...tried to...your wife...he forced her...forced her to...'

For a moment the silence became deafening. Theseus released Oenone, who shrank back: a sweeping score that they could not hear swept into existence, and the floor shook with a bass rumble as buzz-saw guitars obscured falsetto vocals which uttered only horror. Theseus' mind went into overdrive: *no no no no this couldn't be true, I've misunderstood, let me find out what she really means, can I utter the question, it's so sick –*

'Aneurin...raped Phèdre?'

She shuddered through her reply. 'Yes.'

It was as if the music that played around them went through a beautifully orchestrated key change. Everything became clearer and a sense of definity, even calm, descended on the scene, in contrast to the music which became epic and climactic. Theseus found himself swelling with rage and disgust, but it was as if he was looking down on himself bursting with fire: some small central piece of Theseus was remaining calm, and it was this part of him that spoke. He could not act rashly. He had to be clear.

'Say it in full to me.'

Oenone ached with love for Phèdre, and she knew what had to be done. If Phèdre was rid of Aneurin, then she would live and love Theseus – she had said it herself – with Aneurin gone, she loved Theseus – and with her living and loving Theseus, Venus is defeated! Her child is free from the curse, the curse that ends with Phèdre shining brightly in victory over a defeated Venus! There was only a small price to pay, and it was one Oenone was willing to sacrifice. She would have to lie to Theseus about his son: lie grossly, yes, but out of necessity. Phèdre would be free. And so she spat out the lie.

'Aneurin raped your wife.'

She was surprised the words did not burn in her throat. Theseus still looked calm, and his temperament scared her.

'Is the child that grows within her Aneurin's?'

'How do you – ?'

'Neptune told me. Is it?'

Knowing it cannot be, that Phèdre is months pregnant already, and that she never coupled with Aneurin, feeling the lie descend upon her like a weighted darkness, Oenone lies: 'Yes.'

The calm temperament began to fade as the seething rage engulfed the calm kernel of Theseus. The music swelled too and became unbearably ecstatic. Someone, somewhere, was enjoying this: and as Theseus imagined a roaring in his ears, it all seemed to make sense. He heard Oenone's words low in the mix, her voice initiated by fear of his changing mood:

'She is Aneurin's. That's why Phèdre's father came…came to take the child.'

'Minos was here?'

She nodded. He continued.

'Makes sense. He comes to cleanse his own race, because he knows I will not. And he left?'

Again she nodded.

'Yes, he is scared to face me. I walked the Styx right to his doorstep, and only turned back for Phèdre.

'If he had harmed her, or her child, I would go back, beat his door down, and destroy him.'

He began to speak more to himself.

'Is this what the gesamkunstwerk meant? A solo of such beauty that it has to be played out? Is that this child…the merging of beauty and violence?'

His mind returned to the bestiality of the situation, and he felt sickened. *No way. No way. This can't be true.* He looked into Oenone's eyes: he saw only pure love for Phèdre. *Oh no. It must be true.*

She saw doubt in him, and knew it would be crushed with just one more repetition.

This time she stuttered over it, feeling guilt rise inside her.

'Your son…raped your wife, thinking you were dead.'

With that stunning confession, Oenone turned away to flee after Phèdre.

I hope I have saved her, she thought, for it was her only hope.

Aneurin lay with his head on Aricie's lap, drawing strength from her.

Phèdre shut herself into the smallest, darkest room she could find.

Theseus spent a few seconds in thought, then spread his arms wide and looked heavenward.

13

The Ferryman stared out into the well of souls, absorbed in the music. He was hearing something special, and wasn't exactly sure what it was – it was new, unique, as if suddenly the gesamkunstwerk had become masterless and diverged into its own beauty at the expense of arranged logic. He spoke to the depths to see if any souls were ready: none surfaced. He thought this strange, for the maddening sound must be maddeningly amplified in the lake's infinite depths, bringing insanity of the soul to the tortured individuals wrestling with themselves in the liquid.

He tried to comprehend the music, but was unable to: his own incomprehension filed back into the gesamkunstwerk, affecting the noise, and the music realised his incomprehension, and decided to show him: the scene became played out before him as if projected like a black and white film onto the lake's calm surface. The light travels through the inky dark liquid, magnifying, illuminating, distorting: as the images played out before him, spreading through the infinite depths, the cursed souls in the lake interact with the imagery, wending their own agony into the picture.

The Ferryman sees all this. He sees all the emotions of all the characters on his stage, his screen, and these come to him almost at once, as his comprehension dawns. The music makes sense to him, but the emotions that result from his private movie are so raw and complicated that he has to speak to the music to describe them, to tell the music how to make itself, although the music already – subtly, subconsciously – plays as a carefully choreographed soundtrack. He is creating a blueprint for the ultimate song, aided by the song itself. An endless loop. The joint effort creates, for an outside observer, some feeling of perfection – not happiness, but perfection, for the two are very different. Perfection is so easily obtainable, but happiness is shimmering, effervescent, elusive. The gesamkunstwerk is playing out the Ferryman's instructions even as it commands him: an eternal loop lasting an infinity of lifetimes, but bound within a nutshell of raging emotions.

He sees all this, and this is what he says into the darkness:

> 'Start with guitar chords. Finger-plucked. Softly, mellow.
>
> 'Enter a monologue (three minutes long). Fade in after sixty seconds.
>
> 'Male voice, middle-aged, approaching a world weariness. Still feels regret over the mistakes of his youth, namely the first girl he ever loved: he hates the way no-one can come close to her in his mind, because she was created to be his perfection, so how can he not love her?
>
> His heart swells whenever a neuron fires and he subconsciously feels her name, remembers her, and

regrets everything that's happened since, and is destroyed by melancholy as he imagines what his life would be like with her now.

'Monologue. Enter strings, haunting, violins. Warbling tape loop (right side) and sycophantic drone (left side). Volume is half that of voice but increases by $1/25^{th}$ at seven second intervals.

'"This is evil it must be evil there is nothing left in this but evil, how can he – what? Mine own son? Evil has taken him and I could not see it: but oh yes I see it now I can see the darkness in him, he who was oh so pure has shown me the dark side of his face, that bastard, he fooled his father so, I raised him, I cherished him, loved him, took care of him, and this is how he repays me? – the woman I love, oh so love, love so dear, her, my love – I will kill him for it, I must, bespoiling my flower, in her perfection and innocence (look! Even then! I did not look into her eyes, she is gone now, but she cannot condemn him to his father's righteous anger! Even her eyes looking at me would betray what I know to be true, so she did not look, because she does not want a family torn asunder, she did not look) and now she carries his child I must reclaim all it is to be my child damn him that monster! Vile! He spits on the Minotaur as an emblem for disfigured lust <generations to come will tell stories of him in the awed tones reserved for that beast> for a new beast has risen within the breast of my child, and like the beast before – I shudder to think it, but yet I must – the beast must be slain, and I condemn him to death and to torture and to pain."

'End Monologue. End guitar.

'Fade strings out in sixteen seconds. Increase volume
of drone; spread to right side, increase pitch. Enter
steel drums, at a slow pace initially. The drums
remind you, a twenty-one year old, single woman,
dressed up for your sister's eighteenth birthday, of
the sound of footsteps behind you, softly clattering
on the asphalt, walking back from the club, it's
twelve-thirty, the sound of footsteps enters your
alcohol-soaked mind and you wonder who it is,
there, behind you, it could be a man, behind me, a
man with a knife, and lust on the mind, he could
grab me, strong arms encircle me, tough hand over
my mouth, wrestle me down, gag me, take me from
behind, I could never see his face, the fear, the
orgasm, the fear, the orgasm, I'd never see his face,
turn round to see his face, turn round – you turn
around and there's nothing behind you.

'Drums build up to a recognisable beat, but the type
of recognition that acid destroys until one day, you
remember when you first heard it, a sickening
psychedelic flashback at the wheel of the car with
the radio tuned to a pirate station and someone
else's kids in the back seat. Drone stops suddenly,
and only in its absence can you remember it being
there. Drone stops and starts in short and long fits:
short, long long, long long, short short, short.
Drone finishes, and you miss it.

'Enter bass. You take care to not have the bass
rhythms rule your life; but its smoothness is too
irresistible, and you obey its hypnotic suggestions.
The bass rolls off your hips, spreads to your
tongue, twists your spine and makes you wish

more people appreciated music with more than just their ears. Bass continues as long as you can live; stops at least a third before your subconscious belief of your lifespan.

'Enter beautiful mess. Guitar; drums; bass; strings; theramin; tape loops; piano; drone; e-bow; synth; every instrument you can lay your blackened hands on. Continue. The beautiful mess is the sound of being caught in fire and knowing it is smoke inhalation that will kill you but finding little comfort in that primary school knowledge as your flesh is flaming and runs down, sullied, to hang your face, your beautiful features that no-one loved you for melted into a disfigured lump, you know it's getting hard to breath as molten flesh runs past your mouth and you suck it in, desperately gasping for breath, you know it's getting harder to breath as you choke on a particularly bitty globule of liquid matter....

'Continue beautiful mess for eight/twelve minutes and arrange it in repeated crescendos endlessly circling back and over to points of frenzied activity and even more frenzied activity. Keep the audience of one always interested but never caring; always emotive but never emotional; always listening but never comprehending.

'Calm beautiful mess; end all instruments except strings and theramin. The two must interact as deaf and blind people struggling to describe the scene in which the beautiful mess fires through your imagination. They do not help you, but record the details in a diary and tape recorder for historians to look upon with muted interest before consigning the details of your pain to a dusty shelf in a warehouse visited only by academics with a penchant for homosexual relations. They do not care about you.

'Enter distorted voices, shouted nineteen foot from a microphone. Words are unrecognisable, yet they say: Go on. Try it. It's only lust. A harmless emotion. Give it a go. You know you want to. Stop being tied down to a Victorian ethos of morality. This is the real world. Go on. Satisfy.

'End voices, strings and theramin. Complete silence. You hear an electrical buzz and a low rumbling. This lasts too long for you.

'Enter cymbals and monologue. Cymbals softly, at first, but increasing in volume as slowly as the realisation you're in love with your best friend. This takes, of course, over a year, and then the cymbals erupt in a blinding, drunken flash of clarity. The fire burns briefly, for perhaps a week, and then you open your mouth, and it's extinguished immediately.

'Male voice. He too is confused, but somewhere inside him there is a spark //// what spark? //// the spark of happiness. A glow from his mind that indicated {feeling or showing pleasure, contentment or joy} there was something, to him, that found a degree of happiness inside himself.

'"choice but can I choose for on the one there is her and her inhumanity which makes me retch and bleed and die and must be ignored and feigned and forgotten and on the other there is him who is so kind and gentle now and so much in love can I choose to say or choose not to say I must be able to

choose and chosen I have I can feel it somewhere
between my gut and my heart there is a decision
that has been made (dare I trust such a decision to
my spleen?) and I know I cannot denounce the
inhuman lust towards me to him he raised me so I
cannot stab him in the back no this is a secret that
is mine and hers and will die with me and her and
someone so great will never know because for him
to know is for him to know the pain of death but to
still live and still breathe so I shall not tell because
it would break his heart and the relationship and
she is bringing a child into the world (let it not be a
cursed beast of passion!) and if I left yes I will
leave for if I left then the passion abates and the
family continues yes I will leave and leave behind
a happy family I will spare him the awfulness of
reality and let him live in ignorance which is of
course bliss and although it is I as a tortured
individual who must leave at least I will not bear
the pain alone for maybe Aricie xxx will come
with me (maybe we can elope and have a mirrored
family: mirrored, yes, but pure) so yes to leave and
then to have two families separate but forever
linked by blood but still two happy families
content only through separation and then yes I
would be happy and so would he and so would my
wife and as for her I don't know I think that
despite myself I still care for her happiness but I
know not what to do."

'End monologue. Fade cymbals out, fade guitar in.
The chord is driving and energetic, the reciprocal
of your energy first thing in the morning. You still
appear beautiful in the morning and the memory of

the night before makes me love you more. But I know you will only hurt me, and that thought hurts me, because I still love you despite this knowledge, and I'll still love you even as you're hurting me, and I love you now, so I speak:

don't turn your back
a knife between the blades
twist it
twisted
help me twist it (further)
blood-red haemoglobin
(deep-rich) red (let it seep)

tear the six-inch
cold stocky-slit steel
from the fullsome folds of flesh
and inter salt between
the fleshy
rifts and sew it sealed
with barbed needles
and chainmail thread
(help me sew it)

'Enter several guitars, bass, drums, piano. The guitar chords play spontaneously off the main guitar – each recording of this song is different; individual; incomprehensible. Each guitar line crosses over each other; itself; looping, falling, reversing, twisting, entwining; the resultant noise is so harmonically beautiful you wish that your thoughts – themselves looping, falling, reversing, twisting, entwining – could create something that beautiful inside your mind, instead of the excesses of miserable fantasy, prone to idolisation. This continues until you find a pattern in your thoughts, the guitar lines, or even in the lace stitching on the tablecloth – can you read lace? Texts are everywhere, but all they say is IN THE DESERT / I SAW A CREATURE, NAKED, BESTIAL, / WHO, / SQUATTING UPON THE GROUND, / HELD HIS HEART IN HIS HANDS, / AND ATE OF IT. / I SAID, "IS IT GOOD, FRIEND?" / "IT IS BITTER - BITTER," HE ANSWERED; / "BUT I LIKE IT / "BECAUSE IT IS BITTER, / "AND BECAUSE IT IS MY HEART."

'End extraneous guitars, bass, piano. Guitar plays a children's nursery rhyme – it does not matter which one, only the innocence is important. A female voice begins to sing, and there is an uncomfortable backing echo that is not her voice, nor her words, but instead some powerful deep-throated voice that plays out through the singing female voice. (You strain to hear what this deep voice says, but you can only comprehend its tone, and it is menacing.)

'"I said it and now I must face the consequences, I accept how much I am damned, because I am now, even if I was not before I have signed and sealed my own tomb, stared down at my own screaming corpse as I nailed the wood plank by plank over my sepulchre. As I saw them both there, standing there, looking at me, I could see one with horror all over him (smelling it all over him like blood diluted over a watery distance in this broken synapse of a world) with horror and then the other, in such innocent incomprehension, I saw them both standing there – so alike, so beautiful, so alike – and then (all of a sudden) I could not tell who was who, I could not see which was my husband (whom I had greatly wronged) and I could not see which was his son (whom I had greatly wronged) and I spoke out to the silence and the awkwardness and the horror and the incomprehension and I spoke to the guilt and it is all that I said because it all that can be said, and I left to be damned, indeed, I embrace my destruction because it is the only thing left for me."

'End drums.

'Fade guitar through complicated riffs. Fade to silence. The song is over.

'Enter monologue. A small child's voice; can't be aged more than three or four. The voice is sexless and contains an innocence the world weeps for. The words cannot be heard by you. Not yet.

'End monologue. Play a heartbroken years' worth of seconds of silence, and still sit waiting.'

The Ferryman finished speaking.

*

While the Ferryman watched the scene, the puppets that partook in it did not have the benefit of the music feeding them their internal monologues. They were all confused, fearful, angry: hurt, in such pain, and ready to lash out. The parties had all split – Phèdre had left, in tears. Aneurin had made an exit as far from her as possible. Theseus had remained, his jaw suddenly set resolutely. He knew what had to be done, how this monstrosity could be rectified.

He spread his arms wide and looked heavenward.

'Hear me, Neptune – your Champion calls upon you.'

A crackling sparked into existence, and again that dark cloud wove itself into embodiment, the dark cloud that signifies the presence of a dark, powerful deity. Music of epic proportions filled the hallway where he still stood. Neptune's brilliant light emanated from the cloud, fusing two extremes of colour in one fantastic display of awesome power. The very walls of the entranceway appeared to ripple as the cloud assumed form: first, muscular legs flexed themselves into solidity, then the cloud spiralled into a recognisable human form. Within seconds, a tall figure stood before Theseus, bristling with anger: the focus around him appeared to change as his domination of the surroundings became complete.

'Yes, Theseus – you have called, and I have come. But beware: the gods are not the playthings of humans. If you have not summoned me to pay the debt I owe you, then my retribution will be terrible. Now: speak.'

'Fear not, Neptune. I have indeed called you here for you to fulfil your debt. Not even in the months of journeying in that timeless place besides the Styx did I call on you, even though I felt your power in the River.

'Those were dark, dark months. But now I have need of your power, because I have been greatly wronged. Neptune, I ask you to avenge me: kill my son.'

He boiled with rage. Asking a god to kill a human would not be a matter of switching the person out of existence, like erasing a tape. It would involve a bloody mutilation of pain and torture: the person would die a death of unimaginable pain. And Neptune was a very powerful god who has been itching to repay his debt to Theseus, and wanted to fulfil it in extraordinary style.

Furthermore, Neptune was angry at Jupiter for interfering in his domain with the plane crash, and determined to show Jupiter his own power and malice.

All this Theseus knew: and yet he still called this wrathful vengeance down upon his own blood.

'Kill my son. Kill that beast of passion. Kill Aneurin.'

Theseus thought it all made some kind of perverse sense. Phèdre's words; Aneurin's guilty face and ambiguous answers; the refusal of eye contact. He had heard the gesamkunstwerk's words about violence and beauty, and now things slotted together. The melding of beauty and violence is what the music desired – the violence of Aneurin and his rape, the beauty of Phèdre and her sexuality – and the being that resulted is the solo of which the Ferryman spoke.

He had said that a solo of such beauty has to be played out, and Theseus understood why: not through poetic notions of beauty for beauty's sake, but simply because the gesamkunstwerk god is as bored and as cruel as the gods that flutter around Theseus' own world. He had been too late to prevent the creation of the solo, and Minos had been prevented from destroying it by fear of Theseus. But now that the solo was playing itself into corporeality, growing itself, he could not cut it short: but he could render its existence clean.

By calling upon the ultimate power of Neptune, he was removing the person that made the solo's existence base. By forgiving and loving Phèdre, he would love his child, and in doing so stop the music from finding out what future there was for rejected lovers to find…

'I hear you.'

If it was possible, Neptune grew even more massive before Theseus, who felt a sharp stabbing pain in his hand. The Mark of Neptune was engraved on his palm.[2]

---

[2]   For more on the Mark of Neptune, see Appendix C.

'This cannot be revoked. The contract on Aneurin's life has been signed with blood.'

Haemoglobin dripped from Theseus' clenched fist into the cloud of blackness that swept up before him, and vanished into nothingness, taking Neptune with it. The contract was indeed sealed with blood, and Theseus turned with a flourish and exited the room, seeking Phèdre. She was to be avenged. So was he.

Aneurin was to die.

14

Theseus angrily stalked the corridors. Where was everyone? The place seemed to empty: he raged down corridors, through rooms, and saw not a soul. He was desperate to find Phèdre and comfort her, to reassure her that everything was going to be okay, to let her know what fate had in store for Aneurin now. He worked himself up into a righteous anger, and prepared to unleash it compassionately in the presence of his wife.

Instead, however, it was Aneurin himself who he encountered. Seeing his child walk out before him, and knowing what he knew, brought the anger to the surface of Theseus, and he screamed a challenge at Aneurin. The child turned around, and the face looked shocked, and then the father swung, and his fist connected, and the son took the blow and span away, spitting blood. He did not defend himself, nor strike back.

'You! Vile adulterer! And yet your face shines bright with the sacred look of virtuousness,' he sneered, 'but now I recognise the heart of a treacherous man.'

'Dad…what…why?'

Aneurin paused to wipe the blood from the corner of his mouth. It stung slightly as saliva dripped into the bloodstream, and a cellular war took place between platelets and salivic germs.

'What is the cause of all this?'

'You hypocrite! You animal!'

Theseus burst in anger, his neck muscles straining, his face turning red as veins stood out and he began to shout himself out of breath.

'How dare you come before me now? I know who you are and what you have done. And I can promise you there is no escape and no release. The frenzied passion you brought to your father's bed...

'There is no punishment for a crime such as yours. No punishment a human can inflict, anyways.'

Theseus sneered at Aneurin again.

'I have called on Neptune, and he will come for you.'

'Phèdre...accuses me of sinful love? The horror is too much...'

His soul is numb. So many unexpected blows fall on him. Words fail him. A soundscape of paranoia and unfettered introspection rang in Aneurin's ears, and he felt angst-lyrics were screaming somewhere in the mix.

For Theseus, however, the gesamkunstwerk was rushing to his ears like blood to his head, and the sonic construct was overflowing with righteous anger, unintentional melodrama, and spite mixed with bile.

They were both listening to the same music that almost swelled into a tangible existence, but did not even reach as far as an audio existence – instead, it hovered just on the edge of their subconsciouses. It fed them their own emotions on a loop: as one became more introspective, the angst-lyrics became louder, almost audible: as the other became angrier, the spite rose from within the bile like scum to the surface of a fetid puddle.

'Traitor! You hoped Phèdre would be a coward...relied on

female silence, female fear, thinking she'd be too terrified to testify...but she is stronger than you think, and now I know who you are...ingrate!'

Aneurin is completely shocked by this. Incomprehension floods across his face: clearly, Phèdre has told Theseus that it was Aneurin who declared love for her, rather than the truth of reality, she chose the inversion of her perversion. Even so, he did not expect Theseus to react with such violence: his jaw hurt, and his ears hurt from the abuse too.

'I'm outraged at so black a lie...I ought to speak the truth to you now,' Aneurin parried, then paused in thought, before offering the thrust, 'But I'll hold back a secret touching you.'

Theseus looked unconvinced at this – rage seeped from every pore of his being, and it was all he could do prevent himself from striking Aneurin again. *Leave that to the gods.*

'Listen, my father! I invite the gaze upon me. Look at me! I am your son! Look at my life: great crimes are heralded by lesser ones. Have I ever wronged you?

'One day cannot change innocence into licentiousness, lust and immorality. Daylight is not more pure than my heart's centre, and yet you see me raptured by unholy love? Father, *look upon me*. Look into yourself. What do you see?'

'I look into you now and I see a corruption hidden beneath your surface. I see through your skin and I see the effect your life has had upon your body. Your ears, damaged by he dust of Apollo; your spleen, gorging itself on its own eccentricities; your mind, circling the thought of violence against beauty; your loins, coursing with lust and rotting through wantonness; and your heart, that blackened crux of your machine, beating your thick blood around you, spreading vile poison into every corner of your being.

'Do not speak to me! May your eyes be cut out to prevent any more of this.

'You want me to look at myself? I see a churlish fool who indulged you far too long. I see now so clearly. Why were you not a player like me in my youth? You have the same genes, and you grew up under a wanton star and a fertile father.

'Now I know why no-one could charm your lusty eyes: they were set on Phèdre, and only for Phèdre. This is why she tried to get you to study abroad. She wanted to spare me from just this.

'This is what I see. Now, wretch, deny what you can. Stir up my anger with more of your falsities! For revenge is out of my hands now, but I want to feel complete satisfaction when your blood is spilled, and I cure my line from unsanitary demented lust!

'Revenge will not be at my hands, but at Neptune's: he will prepare something in his infinite power, and you will suffer the wrath of a thousand and one lifetimes!'

Theseus' chest heaved with emotion.

Aneurin cast his eyes up from the floor.

He spoke quietly to his father.

'I love Aricie. Not Phèdre.'

Theseus exploded in apoplectic rage again.

'You feign a love to deny your crime? You do not know what love is…only lust.'

Exasperated. 'Will nothing tear you from your fallacies?'

'Get out. The foulness within you infects this place, as a cancerous plague eats its way out from the point of infection, consuming all that is good by turning flesh on flesh as cells attack each other. That is what is happening here. Be gone!'

Aneurin spoke calmly again, having accepted that Theseus' temper would not be calmed today, and whatever crime he was accused of would stick with him for the foreseeable future until the truth could reveal itself, like dawn rising warmth onto a waste land. He had to wait for his father to reach the gloaming before he could see the truth.

He decided to give Theseus' world one last spin to encourage dawn to rise quicker.

'You speak of incest and adultery. It makes my heart break...but I must be quiet. But Phèdre's mother, now...Phèdre...is from a race much fuller in these horrors than my own...'

His voice trailed off.

'You are insane! I see you for the last time. Be gone from my sight!'

Aneurin made to speak in return, but knew it was useless.

He glanced at the window on his way out.

Light streamed through, but there was no sign of dawn for Theseus.

Theseus watched his son go, and something within him felt a twinge of guilt. This was his own flesh and blood he was condemning...that feeling settled heavily on his stomach. His body racked with pain for his son, and his son's crime.

But Aneurin had forced him to it. What father has ever been so outraged? His pain was visible for all to see: can he ever have given life to such a foul child?

'A god of vengeance follows you now as you walk to certain death!' He called after his departing son. 'At the river that even the gods fear, Neptune gave me his favour, and now I have his word upon the task! I loved you once, but you won't escape!'

Aneurin heard little of this, as he had already exited, and was running away. Another spectator heard the end of the speech, though, as she entered the room through a different exit merely seconds after Aneurin had left.

Theseus did not notice her as he shouted after his son, and it was only when she pulled the curtain over the window and plunged the room into darkness that he became aware of her presence. She spoke first, unsure of events that had already taken place.

'I'm terrified – '

'Don't be, everyth– '

'No…I've heard the awful things you said, and I fear that your threat will soon be carried out. Please: if there is still time left, spare your child. Don't let me hear his anguished cries, do not place his destruction at my door. Don't let me be the cause of a father letting blood flow.'

'My hands are free from him. There will be no blood on my conscience: I have charged Neptune with it, and he has heard my prayer. Look!'

He held his hand up to Phèdre, and she could see Neptune's mark cut onto Theseus' palm, and she knew the blood had sealed the pact, and that nothing could save Aneurin's life. She had played her part in the death of the man she loved: he was a dead man walking. She went silent through grief. Theseus continued his tirade, his being bristling with righteous anger.

'Stir up my hatred against him. Give me the darkest details of his crime. Exorcise the demons: tell me about his baseness, the inhumanity, the sordid lust – tell me about the incident.'

His baseness? His?

'Stir up my anger, gone too slow and stale, against the ingrate. And yet you do not know all his wickedness! He lied to me, claimed purity, and insulted you, and your name, and professed a love pure and natural in the face of so much evidence!'

Phèdre was no longer listening to Theseus' words.

What had given him that impression? Certainly Aneurin would not have told Theseus that lie…who else knows? Oenone, dear Jupiter…was it Oenone? Did she proclaim a lie on my behalf? And why?

To try and save me?

Oh, poor, sweet, precious Oenone, how little she understands…she has got involved and condemned my precious Aneurin to death…

She half-heard something and snapped back to attention.

'...yes, that foul beast claimed a sanctity that was not his, claiming a real and true love with her!'

'Her?' Phèdre questioned automatically.

'With Aricie!'

So Aneurin loves, but not me; and Aneurin will die, without me.

And jealousy exploded from outside her body to make Phèdre surge passionately, violently, and then her body collapsed beneath her green-hued mind as she fainted straight out onto the floor.

15

She came to with her face sideways on a black sofa. The room appeared on end: chairs and tables floating on the left-hand side of her periphery vision, eerily suspended from gravity. It took her a second to comprehend her sensory input, and then her mind flooded back: that hussy Aricie had captured her Aneurin.

Her mind bled with jealousy. How they must enjoy themselves…the candlelit dinners…the long walks by the sea, freely moving between the cool, dark forest and the bright, hot sunshine of the coast…how they were able to laugh, and giggle…how they made love without guilt…how the passion for them was free…heaven approved their innocent desires! Each day dawned for them, so cloudless, so serene…

meanwhile
here I hide
from daylight
from sunshine
and night

for he will never be mine…

Dear god! Aneurin! He is condemned to death…a god of vengeance stalks him…the mark of Neptune is placed on his head by his father's hand…and why? Because of lies! Damned, detested lies! Oenone…it must have been her…she will pay for her crime…she has killed my love, my liege, my heart's only desire, she has murdered him…there is blood on her hands…

Phèdre sat up, and the world righted itself. Next to her on the sofa was a tearful Oenone. She spoke first while Phèdre listened with a becalmed silence.

'My lady! I am so glad you're okay. Your husband has gone to plead at Neptune's altar for a swift and bloody revenge. My lady, you are safe…as is your secret with me…you can live, and be free – free from guilt as this is not by your hands, and free from Venus' curse!'

Silence. Then:

'How little you understand, Oenone. I am not free, not free at all: my soul is chained in grief. And it is all your fault!'

'My lady?'

'Yes, Oenone, it is all your fault,' said Phèdre as she stood up and drew herself up to full height, 'it is your fault that Theseus now prays for the death of my beloved. It is your fault a god of vengeance stalks the beat of my heart. It is his blood that is on your hands.'

Oenone stood.

'My lady, what is it you say? I have saved you…your love is our secret now, and you can live on with Theseus.'

'I do not want to live on! Without Aneurin, there is no life! I can never forgive you this crime. You sicken me! You have destroyed me!

'I wish you dead, and if I ever see you again, it will be too soon.'

Oenone was shocked: she looked at Phèdre storming out of the room, and saw the reason for her existence leave with the violent slamming of the door. She sat down heavily, deathly thoughts cascading through her consciousness, and immediately hot tears welled up in the corners of her eyes, and she put her hands to her head, and wept.

Suddenly, she felt an arm around her, and she screamed and jumped up in shock – she had not heard anyone come in. She pivoted about to look down on the sofa, and was surprised to see a tall, dark, handsome man sitting there, smiling serenely at her.

'Who are you?'

'Hi. I'm Minos,' he said, standing up and offering his hand, 'you must be Oenone. I really must thank you for your hard work with Phèdre, I do appreciate it, really I do.'

'Minos? But…you don't…look like that…'

'Ah, but I do, my dear…what did you expect? Horns and a forked tail? My love, evil is much better hidden in the heart of the smart corporate businessman or in the numbers on a balance sheet. Be assured, I am Minos.'

'Why are you here? Last time you came…you came to kill Phèdre! Monster!'

He sighed, and put his hand down. He had the air of a kindly school teacher explaining the way of the world to a child.

'You misunderstand me. I did not come to kill her, for I am not a murderer. She desired death: I came to supply it. A father always tends to the needs of his child. But Oenone, dear, why does this bother you? Let us not forget that she just disowned you, wished never to see you again, and wished you dead.'

The truth of the situation hit Oenone again, and she wept. Minos stepped forward and embraced her: he felt warm, and his shoulders were broad, and Oenone buried herself in him, drew strength from him, cried until her eyes ached, cried until the tears almost became bloody. And all the time: Minos whispered to her, into her ear, telling her that Phèdre had disowned her, and how he knew his Phèdre better than even Oenone, and how this would not be revoked, and how Oenone's purpose in life had fettered away, and how her life was not empty and devoid of meaning, and that, really, she'd be better off dead, then she would be with him, and he could finally repay her for the kindnesses she had shown his daughter, and he spoke all this softly, with a serpent's tongue, and it greased the ear of Oenone, and slipped into her consciousness, and she began to believe it: she wished for death already, but her natural tendency to endure (men must endure their going hence even as their coming hither: that ripeness of spirit is all) blocked her suicidal thoughts, but in the strong arms of Minos, Oenone gave herself over to her dark thoughts and entered a suicidal spiral of depressive thinking.

'Come…' Minos uttered to her.

He could see the machinations at work in her mind, feel the emotions course through her body, and he knew when she was ripe for plucking. He led her out to the balcony, and viewed the marvellous vista.

'Phèdre no longer wants you. *But I do.*'

Oenone repeated, 'Yes, Phèdre no longer wants me. I thought I would wander the globe unloved forevermore: thought that each of my days henceforth would live out a hollow lie, an empty existence floating in the mayhem and chaos of this world.

'I wished for death just yesterday: wished it as I saw Phèdre wither away before my eyes. I could not live a life without Phèdre. And I cannot now.'

Her words sparked a grin in Minos, and looking into his comforting features, she breathed, 'see you soon,' and leapt over the balcony.

She hurtled towards the waves that seemed to reach up, tiny wave-fists grabbing, clutching at her body, so that as she hit the surface, and went beneath, she was pulled on downwards, steadily away, pulled down into the Sea's bosom, where the life was choked from her, and she did not even have enough breath to scream Phèdre's name in the middle of her instant regret.

On the balcony, a shattering black light cracked, and where the handsome man had stood, Minos stood in his true form: massive and dominant, horns whelked and waved like the enraged sea, chuckling quietly to himself. It was good to get out once in a while.

16

'So he thinks that I…that I…'

Aneurin shuddered to complete the sentence. Aricie, however, already knew what he meant.

'But why? Who would have told such a lie?'

'Only four people know her blackness: you, me, herself, and Oenone. Phèdre would not commit this sin. It must be Oenone.'

'You cannot be so sure…Phèdre is guilty of worse crimes. It is only a small step to this outrage from her last one…it is only the blackening of your name to save her existence, her marriage, her family…'

'No…her crime consumes her, abhors her…she could not increase the guilt upon her own head. Self-loathing fills her, just as it fills me…you can see it in her eyes, just as she can see it in mine.'

'So you think it's Oenone?'

'Yes. Not that it matters…the lie is out there, forced into existence, and with a smattering of truth, it has become even more believable. Theseus has no reason not to believe it…it makes sense to him…why else would Phèdre shun me?

'The reality – that she both shuns and worships me – is lost upon him, and his jealous pride, which so ruled his lustful youth, rises from the ashes of his son's decency. He believes the lie. And now a god of vengeance stalks me.'

'What will you…us…what will we do?'

'We must flee, and pray that the gods have a bone of kindness in their bodies. They cannot allow this tragedy to unfold…one amongst them must shine down upon us, and counter the Mark. One god will be fair.'

Aneurin was suddenly, against his will, reminded of his conversation with Aricie in a London restaurant. Was it really only two days ago?

'Where can we flee from the gods?'

Aneurin wracked his brain in thought.

'The Vault!'

'What?'

'Remember? The Vault of the Gods?'

'Oh yeah…' Aricie breathed with understanding.

'There, anyone who swears a falsity is instantly erased, burnt from reality through an outpouring of outrage. Anyone who swears falsely before the eyes of the gods is destroyed by the haunting, omnipresent music that is there. Theseus did not marry Phèdre there, for he had already wed Ariadne before the gods: a second marriage is considered adultery. Only true, first love can be sworn there, for the music will smite the unjust who perjure in their presence. It is there that the Mark can be lifted…for there, the son of Theseus will die, and be reborn as husband of Aricie.'

'What…?'

Aneurin bent a knee.

'Aricie…come away with me. Let's elope. Will you marry me?'

Her head span: her heart beat: her eyelids flickered: her lungs expanded: the moment froze.

She felt her heart would burst as it struggled to move the volume of blood about her trembling body.

This was so crazy.

But so right.

She realised she loved Aneurin, and had to spend the rest of her life with him.

She could not bear his death.

'Yes. I love you.'

Aneurin shattered in relief, his legs turning to jelly as he stood up and swept her into his arms, and they kissed. He wasn't even that worried about her reply: a part of him knew, just knew she was going to say yes.

'I love you, too.' They kissed again. He didn't want to go, but knew that time was running out. Neptune stalked him.

'Meet me at the temple before dusk…I have to prepare the ground, incense and all that. Bring only what you cannot leave behind. We will never see this place again.'

He kissed her goodbye, and left.

Aricie stood watching her fiancé leave, staring at the door through which he had exited. She sat down heavily, and felt her face flush with happiness. She was almost breathless with excitement, with exhilarated energy, and she could not wait to meet Aneurin in this temple, and swear her undying love to him. She sat for a few minutes enjoying the anticipation. She had no fear of falsity in that place: she loved Aneurin so entirely that she would not be struck down.

She leapt up, giggling, and turned round.

The colour drained from her face as her mood evaporated.

Theseus strode into the room, murderous anger etched onto his face.

He spoke first to her. 'You! Why do you associate yourself with people of that calibre?'

He practically spat.

'I suppose you applaud incest, and cheer at adultery,' he sneered, 'my son makes me sick, but at least I no longer willingly associate myself with him. We share a surname, but that is all that links us. But you...you...you willingly align yourself to him. Do you know the darkness of his crimes?'

'I love him.'

'And I bet he has sworn his love to you, too. Do you know how many others he has sworn his love to? And how many more he has taken? Taken!'

Theseus' anger began to tire, to wilt before Aricie's composed visage. There was something inside her which made him halt. He looked into her eyes, and saw:

floating on the white, her belief that he was mistaken
    (harmonious string quartet implies a world being shaken)
swimming in the green, her belief that Aneurin was innocent
    (stirring bass pounds the realisation of an honesty bent)
present in the black, her desire for the truth

He paused. His anger had blown itself out. He looked into her eyes, and doubted himself. He let her speak. She spoke with an authority and self-belief that frightened him.

'Can you so little tell a crime from innocence? Repent your murderous prayers. Fear lest the gods feel harsh, and grant your rash request.'

'You're...blinded by love...' he meekly offered by way of argument.

'No, my lord, it is you who are blinded by love. You are Champion of Neptune, you have freed mankind from countless monsters, but not all have been destroyed. One remains. You son…forbids me to speak of it. I know how much he loves you, which is why I remain silent. I must leave you now, before I'm made to speak…'

'No! You will not leave!'

Theseus snapped into action. Aricie's words worried him: her belief in herself and Aneurin tortured him. She had to be made to speak.

'You will not leave until you have told me what you know. Speak!'

'My lord, I cannot…now I must go…' She made to leave, and Theseus saw a chance of the truth going with her. He restrained her, and she had no choice but to bow to his strength and wait while he called for his bodyguards. Two men arrived as if from nowhere, and he spoke to them.

'Do not allow her to leave.'

He turned to Aricie.

'Now you are a prisoner until you tell me what you know.'

He saw tears form in her eyes. The water only magnified the intensity of her self-belief in her eyes. She sat back down heavily, defeatedly, and spoke quietly.

'Ask Oenone for the truth.'

She broke into sobs, and could not be tempted to talk through tears.

'You there!' Theseus addressed one bodyguard. 'Go fetch Oenone. We must solve this mystery.'

From within him, an intense feeling of unease began to grow.

He had Aricie taken away, for she had collapsed into an insensible lump of a wreck. It was as if some overpowering lethargy had stolen all her energy: she no longer had the strength for tears. But she could not be persuaded to talk, so Theseus had her locked in Aneurin's room, lain on his bed for her safekeeping. He could not let her go, for she had some part to play in this.

The bodyguard was gone an hour; two. How long could it take to find Oenone? Theseus broke into a cold sweat. *Could I be mistaken?*

Panopé is brought into the room, manhandled by the bodyguard. Her body language shows she is broken: tear-marks streak her face, and she is limp all over.

'Panopé...what...where is Oenone?'

At the name, fresh tears flowed.

'She's dead, m'lord...she killed herself.'

The news settled heavily on Theseus' stomach as his feeling of unease broke around his whole body.

'How?'

'She drowned...the sea seemed intent on swallowing her up...she leapt from the balcony in Phèdre's quarters, and I saw her, jumping...the sea took her straight down to its bed, seductively, on a path of unrivalled calm, while the waters surged around her, and she swirled in her own misery and despair...there was something unnatural about it...the eerie calm...how she sunk like a stone...'

The news hit Theseus hard. He flooded with doubts, but let Panopé continue.

'And as if that suicide is not bad enough, now my mistress is muttering about it too...'

This latest news was too much for Theseus. He thought about Oenone's suicide, and Phèdre's desperation: nothing made sense anymore. He must take time to re-instate the order of the world. He regretted his rashness, a hangover from his lusty youth. He had to halt Neptune's revenge until he was sure.

He spread his arms and looked into the sky.

'Hear me, Neptune, your Champion calls on you.'

Nothing happened.

'Neptune! It is I, Theseus!'

Silence.

'Delay your revenge! Agh!'

With the last command, Theseus felt a stabbing, burning pain. He looked at his hand: the Mark was bleeding.

The deal had been signed with blood.

17

It is a bright sunny afternoon, and there is a slight breeze coming from the sea onto the shore. Aneurin is eloping to the temple, romantically taking a horse-drawn carriage, complete with the family coat of arms and ceremonial spear, along the cliff-tops to the Vault of the Gods. These are the horses he grew up with, he reflected, horses that he trained with while he was still in Athens. He remembered them, the beautiful Pegasus and Tristar, training in the dust, in the dark forest, in the sweltering heat before the palace...he urged them on.

It had taken longer than expected to gather the incense and religious tomes, and chant the necessary incantations, and prepare the horses: but now he was on his way to the temple, and he hoped Aricie had not already arrived. He wasn't far away now...there, over that hill, there was a concealed entrance. The location of the Vault was a strict secret: only members of the Royal family knew where it was, it was said that no-one else could find it, unless a member of the Royal family told them where it was.

He arrived a few moments later. Bracken covered the entranceway: Aricie had not arrived yet. He hacked away at it, and descended into the darkness after tying up the horses and gathering a torch. He felt nervous, and it wasn't just wedding jitters. Something about the place was entirely spooky. He descended down steep stone steps, darkness flickering away around him. Then: he heard it.

Some mournful music played, and he thought he could hear whispered vocals, speaking what may have been Essil. The music made him feel ill, but he continued on, down and down, the passageway spiralling in a clockwise direction. What did that mean?

Finally he emerged into an underground vault, and the space was empty, save for an altar at one end of the room. He felt a chill pass down his spine as he felt the music tell him that it was both a marriage altar and a sacrificial table. Aricie's love would decide which it was to be.

He threw off his doubts, and lit the incense. He chanted the correct words in Essil that he read from the various religious books he brought with him. The site was prepared. There was a unearthly presence tinged in this place: the music had no source, and could not be stopped. He thought perhaps it was his own mind that was creating it, and with that thought, the music changed. Did he influence that change in the music, or did the music influence his change of mind?

He looked at his watch, and waited. Aricie was already late.

*

The Ferryman stood before the Well of Souls, and shook his head. So sad...a melancholy note sprang up within the gesamkunstwerk as the tragedy began to play itself up. He could hear the desperation in the air...could hear the combined tears of Phèdre and Aricie played out as falsetto backing vocals...could hear the combined worry of Aneurin and Theseus wend itself into the music as electrical buzzes...the Ferryman shook his head again.

'So sad.'

They were the first words to be uttered in the Well of Souls since the Ferryman's vision. He had stopped asking if souls were ready to surface and travel to Hades: none answered, but at the sound of his voice, one rotting corpse surfaced, its head breaking the smooth glass-like surface, and rose up, and the Ferryman realised the figure that approached was Oenone.

She felt her way to shore: she was blind. He saw muddy blood drip from her eyes. She had been so beautiful. Now she was scarred by violence, scarred by the mistakes of her soul. Spasms of pain rendered themselves through the gesamkunstwerk: sudden excessively loud bursts recorded Oenone's discomfort. The Ferryman had no choice. He swept up onto his boat, and took Oenone by the hand, and sat her down. He cast off to the other bank, gliding on the silken smooth surface of the dark underground lake. The boat approached the other side, and the Ferryman saw the door of blackness wreathed in flame.

The entrance to hell stood open, and Minos stood beside the door, beckoning her onwards. This she could not see, but the music built up her notes of panic: shifting time signatures scared her even more, and the Ferryman placed her on the opposite shore, and Minos took her by the hand, and led her into hell.

'So sad,' the Ferryman uttered again. This time no souls rose, although the volume of the music did.

*

Aricie, locked in Aneurin's quarters, thinks she hears music play somewhere close by. She needs to get out. Aneurin is waiting for her, she is going to be late for her wedding. Worse, she does not know if she can arrive at all. It is beginning to darken. It means she is really late. But maybe, under cover of darkness, she can escape – it may be possible to climb out the window, for Aneurin's quarters are not far from the ground. It's worth a try, she muses, as she knots bedsheets together. By the time she has a rope long enough to reach, the sun is setting, and she climbs out the window. She has to make her way to Aneurin. What must he be thinking?

*

She isn't coming, he thought. *Why did she agree to marry me if she wasn't going to come?* He became consumed with doubts. *She doesn't love me enough to swear it here, where she could die from a falsity. Perhaps she isn't sure she loves me enough to swear here. Maybe she only said yes because I said it is the only way for me to be saved from Neptune. And that's true...but given time to think about it...she's backed out...now we won't marry here, live a happy life...all that happiness, gone...I am rejected, a reject...a rejected lover...*

He blew out the candles and incense, and headed back upstairs into the light. He saw the sun was close to setting. He had to return to the palace, and find Aricie, and find out what had gone wrong. He didn't care about the Mark, or that Aricie was the only way to save him: he only gave a damn about his relationship with her. For if there was none, then it didn't even matter if Neptune had Marked him. Life wasn't worth living.

He untied the horses, and set off back to the palace at a fierce pace. It is not long before he sees the palace looming before him in the rising twilight, and he notes with a vague impatience that the sea is becoming heavier, that there is a rustling wind, and that the twilight is lasting an unnaturally long time.

Then, with a heaving and a bursting, and an earthquake which moved the very ground he stood upon, a gigantic tidal wave scoops out onto the path before him: his horses rear up, frightened. Before him stands a monster plucked straight from the depths of the ocean: twelve feet tall, muscles rippling, the half-man half-beast breathes fire from every enormous nostril, his eyes blood red, horns jagged and dangerous, dripping with infection, his yellow skin caked with scales. Aneurin screams, and the monster lumbers forward with surprising agility. He leaps forward from his carriage, grasping the ceremonial spear from the side: every inch his father's son, Aneurin knows he must defeat this monster of Neptune. It stands awash in the foam, like some hell-hound or untamed bull, and then charges upon Aneurin.

He rolls to one side.

The beast blunders past, destroying the carriage with a massive fist.

Aneurin stabs the spear through the underside of the beast's jaw.

There is a roar of pain, and the monster hits out in anger, connecting with Aneurin and sending him flying into the wreckage of his chariot. The beast dances about in pain.

*

131

Aricie runs from the palace: she has not got far, and she feels uneasy in the unusually long twilight. She knows it is a long way to the Vault of the Gods, but Aneurin will still be there for her, he must, else he will be heading back to her, and they will meet on the way.

Aricie felt the ground shake.

She comes over the crest of the hill and is met by the most astonishing sight. There is Aneurin, facing a beast conjured from the depths of the ocean, a dozen arms waving with unbridled strength and malicious evil. He stands alone before this beast, and she screams as she sees it charge at him, and watches helpless, crying out, as he rolls beneath its reach, then stabs it with a spear, and is caught by one of the fists and knocked into the wreckage of his carriage, and sees the beast dance in pain, and sees his anguished movements frighten the horses, who bolt, and sees the slack in the reigns gathering movement, and then sees Aneurin caught in the leather ropes, being dragged off, as the beast succumbs to its injury, roaring in agony, spurring the horses on in fright, and Aricie is sure she can see a god digging its heels into their dusty flanks as they disappear over the next hill into the distance, dragging Aneurin behind them, through sharpened, jagged rocks, she can see him collide with them at full speed, see vibrant red blood splatter onto the rocks, sees him disappear over the horizon as she cries and runs uselessly after them.

18

The apartment is empty. Aricie has gone. A trail of knotted bedsheets leads to the window: she has escaped, and gone to her lover. Theseus sits down heavily. His blood pressure rises as he contemplates his mistake: he feels as if his arteries have turned into welts, burning flesh swelling the passageways, raising the blood pressure, suffocating his mind. Through the haze of worry and self-pity that clouds his mind: he must find Aricie. He realises that it is almost impossible for Phèdre to be pregnant with Aneurin's child, for Neptune told him of the conception before the incident happened. Allegedly happened, he ruefully realised. He damned his return to the rash attitude of his youth.

A mad dash ensues: she will have left the palace: he must leave the building too: he heads towards the entranceway, the theatre-like sculpture hewn into the palace's grandiosity, and tumbles down the stairs in a panicked haste. The monochromatic colour scheme appeared to darken in the twilight: an unusually long twilight, he mused, as he reached the bottom of the steps.

But then: a figure approaches, and stops him in his haste.

'Phèdre?'

She is swarthed in black garments, and looks pale. She staggers towards him, and speaks slowly, as if each word pains her.

'Theseus…listen to me.'

He goes to speak.

'No…listen to me.'

He obediently holds his tongue.

'I have been cursed since before you knew me. I was unaware of this curse, or at least unaware of the strength of it: I knew it would come, but I also knew I was strong. I thought I could defeat it. You know the curse of which I speak: Venus has caused me to burn.

'It was decided before I was born…as well you know. Ariadne burned for you: and Venus destroyed her. I thought I burned for you, and thought I had banished Venus, for she had not destroyed me. But her power is real. And it took me, against my will.

'Do not blame Oenone. She was trying to help me. Her misguided, blind love destroyed us. She told you a falsity: Aneurin is innocent. Far more innocent than you can imagine.'

'So there was no rape?'

'Rape? No...he was too innocent, too pure...which will be why Venus chose him for this.'

'What have I done?!'

'You should worry about what I have done. I tried to foil her...I burned incense, worshipped at her altar, intoned her name...still she made me burn with passion.

'I tried to shun it. That's why I had you send him away! Damn Venus. And you, my poor, sweet husband...Venus has ruined you twice.'

'That'll be the only way Jupiter let her play this out. He hates Neptune, and he hates me.'

Phèdre gave a gasp of pain. Theseus went to speak, but she

talked over him.

'No...listen. My time is not long for this world. I can feel the poison flowing through me: it is time an earthly concoction flowed through me, rather than the dusty emotions of the deities. I am dying, Theseus, but I must put all my mistakes into order.

'I am destroying Venus' curse, for it dies with me: I am pregnant with your child, and I am sorry you will never see her. But she will never burn before Venus' altar, and although I fear death as I will have to stand before my father – think of the tortures he will inflict on his own kind! – I find some comfort that I have destroyed Venus' curse, as my daughter will not worship at her altar. I am devastated that my daughter will not be born, but I find relief that Venus' curse ends with me.'

Finally Theseus spoke without Phèdre silencing him.

'Our child is not a girl. Neptune told me: a future king grows in your belly.'

Comprehension dawned in Phèdre's darkening eyes. Already the poison had cooled her extremities as she felt her heart slow and the blood froze away from her central body warmth. She collapsed onto the floor: both in shock, and as the poison took its cancerous affect.

'A boy?'

'Yes.'

'Then Venus' curse ends with me anyway...my child would not worship at her altar...there would be no sacrifices...no guilty self-torture...the curse ends with me. It was all in vain to try and defeat Venus! All she wanted was to destroy me...then her revenge would be complete...she will re-awaken as a deity of power.

'It was all in vain. We are the gods' playthings. Now Venus! You have your victory! I hope you are happy!'

She broke into tears. Theseus noted her breath fogged the air: her tears turned to ice as the poison worked its deadly magic, cooling her body, bringing icy death to the heart that burned with unearthly passion. She reached for his hand as she lay on the floor. It was cold to the touch: it almost froze their flesh together. 'I am gone from this world. Theseus…forgive me…I cannot see this world…the darkness falls like a mist…father, I come…'

He felt her grip loosen.

He saw her fogged breath evaporate into nothingness.

The grief burst forth from his heart, tears came from his eyes.

There was darkness in her unmoving eyes.

Theseus hunched over the body, his tears flowing from his eyes, flowing with abandonment, with complete disregard for dignity, to drip on the corpse of his wife.

He buried his face in his hands, and wept, and wept, and wept.

He opened his eyes in his hands. The Mark burned bright with blood in the darkness he created around his eyes. Immediately he remembered his son: how a god of vengeance stalked him: and how he must remove the Mark now he knew his son's innocence. He looked at his wife's body, looked into her darkened eyes, but found he could not curse her for her part in this orgy of miscommunication. He still loved her. And he still loved his son.

He knew the way the Mark worked. He needed to find Aneurin, and protect him from Neptune's curse: if it cannot be lifted, maybe it can be defeated. He did not get his Championship of Neptune lightly: he has battled gods before, and won – he can do it again, and if not, he will die trying, and that is enough to satisfy the Mark.

If the Mark cannot be lifted, then a sacrifice will have to be made: if it is to be either him or Aneurin, then it must be him. All this was his fault: he remembered the Ferryman's words, that his presence sparked the greatest solo in the gesamkunstwerk. He had sparked this into motion. He must save his son.

He immediately fled the darkened entranceway, burst out into the open air, the dusk still settling heavily around him. It was still twilight. Theseus fled from the body of his wife, running into the dusk, wildly, compassionately: he saw shapes and figures in the grounds, but none of them were Aneurin, nor Aricie.

Theseus felt the earth quake.

The ground shook, and the palace collapsed. Black and white stones crumbled, crashed down on each other, as a grey rubble threw up a cloud of dust. Then Theseus heard something that went right through him.

An almighty roar rendered the twilight silence: he had heard such a sound before, several times before, but only from one thing, one type of thing: he heard the sound, and he knew: he knew that the noise had come from a beast, a beast of the gods, plucked from the infernal depths, for he had slain so many beasts of that ilk, but he heard the noise, and he was worried, for Neptune's revenge was flooding forwards, and he snapped his head around to the direction the noise came from, and he saw silhouetted on the top of a hill Aricie, and he heard the beast roar again, and as he set out, running, towards the commotion, he heard Aricie scream, and then she disappeared from his sight as he ran.

*

The beast's dying roars frighten the horses, and they bolt, but their reigns are still tied to the remains of the carriage, now splintered by Neptune's strength, and Aneurin is lying on broken wood, and he cannot see the beast, but he swivels around to see it, to continue the fight, and just as his eyes move around enough to see the beast collapse in its fatal throes, the slack in the reigns is gathered up by the galloping horses, and those beasts run frightened and amok, and he is jerked after them, the snap of his acceleration hurting his neck, and then the ground rushing past his body, burning, scraping, cutting, and dust is in his eyes, and he cannot see, and he screams in pain, and then calls out to the horses to calm them, to Pegasus and Tristar, who he trained, and loved, and loved him, but their fear increases, and they run hard and fast as sweat foams in their flanks, and still the painful ground rushes past, and then the beasts enter rocky land, and Aneurin is still dragged behind them, and with sickening crashes he connects with rocks, the first one he smashes into shatters his left leg, and he looks down through dusty, bloody eyes and he can see the bone sticking out, there is a splintering of marrow, and agony is all his mind can register, but then he hits another rock, dragged on by the horses' fear, and he flies into the air, but lands on a jagged rock, so sharp it punctures a lung like a knife, and then a deep gouge is ripped through his back, and he screams, and the horses change direction, and he swings out behind them, and his head connects with the solid stone, his eye is smashed out, and still the horses run, and there are stones, and they are jagged, and he collides with them, each new collision causing further damage, as more limbs break, his spleen is ruptured, the agonies, each new collision is pain, and pain, and pain, and still the horses run, and Aneurin's body is broken, and he struggles with consciousness, but something beyond him prevents him slipping away from his agony, and his senses do not dull themselves, but he can feel each new injury as it occurs, the breaking of a broken body, as still the horses race on, their hooves beating out a rhythm, and each connection with a rock shatters like a cymbal, and broken limbs are broken further, and painful incisions rip chunks of flesh from him, and yet his consciousness remains, and then finally the horses slow, they have run until they feel safe, and then they stop, and finally Aneurin rests in a bloody mess, disfigured and in agonies, mud and dirt and dust caked into his injuries, and the pain floods up about him, and he lies totally broken before the twilight sky, and his mind, broken and with bits missing, his mind realises that he is dying, and he has so many final thoughts that all distil themselves with rapid precision, as he realises what is important to him in his life, as the agonies flare up, he realises his physical pain is unbearable, but it is nothing in comparison to his emotional distress, as he lies with a broken mangled corpse for his body, he realises that the pain of Aricie not meeting him is worse, so much worse, and that he has been rejected by his lover, and that she got cold feet for the wedding, that he was never truly loved, it was all a big deception, and he squirmed to split blood, he saw through bloody eyes that vomit trickled from a hole in his stomach, that Aricie only agreed to marry to his face as she didn't want his death, but that it was not love, at least not from her, he gagged on blood, and she could not swear before the gods because she never loved him that much, it was all a kind of cruel game to her, and his eyes tried to cry tears but only succeeded in bringing blood down the tear duct, and blood came from his eyes, as he felt himself slip away from this world, which held nothing for him as a rejected lover, that was empty for him as Aricie did not return his feelings, and he felt the twilight begin to fade into blackness, and his pain began, finally, thankfully, to dull, and he thought after his father, and his father's wife, and how they made it past the stage of rejected lovers, but it never stopped them returning to the state, perhaps it is the natural human state, as he realised that the truth would out itself in the wake of his death, and he knew his father would be consumed by guilt, as would Phèdre, and Aricie, and he uttered a prayer for them, but found his jaw was broken and disfigured and he could not move it, not that it mattered as his tongue was a stump, bitten through by his own teeth as his agony was inflicted, and he could only pray in his mind, which was beginning to bleed, and he asked for forgiveness for them, and he prayed that they could be happy, even Aricie who tortured him in his last few moments, and he hoped that she would be happy again and his death would not hurt them too much, and he suddenly spasmed as his vertebrae finally gave way, and a horse walked past his fading eyesight, grazing unconcernedly on the grass, and the pattern of foamy sweat looked like a face on its flank, and the face looked cruelly happy, and he realised with a sinking of his stomach that Neptune is god of horses as well as the sea, and they were his instruments in his own death, and his head fell to one side and saw his arm, bent at a broken angle so his hand was right up there next to his eyes, which saw nothing but blackness, and then as his mind started to close itself, the one eye that could still focus saw something glowing, and with his dying energy, he forced it to focus on his hand, and there before him, etched on his own broken hand, was the Mark of Neptune, and he knew his death was at the hands of Neptune, then he surged one final time for Aricie, and blood dripped from his eye as he remembered he was a rejected lover, and that was his last thought, as he heard music, a harmonious beauty, as his breath leaves his body, his overworked mind finally shuts down, then his body, now empty and devoid of soul, his eyes finally without fire, his body, a mangled mess, lying in the twilight, his body emptied of soul lying in the twilight, a musical score fading from his uncomprehending ears.

*

Aricie runs after her departing lover. She sees the blood spattered, vibrantly, despairingly, over the rocks, and her heart is in her mouth as she fears for her lover. Lactic acid courses through her veins: tears are in her eyes: her lungs burn. She passes the twitching body of the beast, a foul odour settling like a haze around the creature, and she does not heed the danger in its fatal spasms, and she ignores its malevolent rage and its dying screams, for she is concentrating alone on Aneurin. She sees the dusty cloud moving off into the distance, pursuing the horizon, as it seeped slowly, tortuously away from her.

She followed the trail of broken grass which disappeared as the ground turned to broken rock: there, however, the trail is clearly marked with red, and she sees chunks of flesh, and her eyes mist with tears, but still she follows the trail of destruction, her trepidation growing with each step, as each step burns her strength, and she is worried.

She passes over the hill-top: the horizon is still out of reach, but in the twilight she sees that the horses have stopped, and Aneurin – is it him? – lies resting on the ground. She shudders to look at him: he is broken. She sees him writhe in pain: a back spasm: his head rolls to one side, and then he is still.

She runs towards him, but everything is in slow motion.

She stands over him, taking in his punctured lung, broken limbs, gouged eye, snapped vertebrae, missing flesh, taking it all in with a single glance, and then she throws herself onto the mangled body, unconcerned that her own clothes are soiled and muddy.

He lies, broken, unmoving in the twilight.

Her head lies on his breast: there is no movement.

She fears.

And his eyes show no life.

Aricie cradles his body before her, crying: blood-hot tears rush down her face as all the emotional agony in the world pours itself forth from her sickened cage. Her grief is uncontrollable as all the emotional pain in the world floods through her, screamed from her mouth, bled from her eyes. And in her mind, a small section which is aloof from the grief: she realises that the last time Aneurin saw her, she agreed to marry him in the Vault of the Gods, and he did not know that she was forcibly detained, he must think that I did not want to come, he must have thought that I had rejected him, that he was jilted at the altar, that he died a rejected lover...

She cradles him in her lap, and screams anger at the gods.

*

The twilight is still lasting, an unnaturally long dusk, eerie and unearthly. Theseus runs past the beast, in pursuit of the horizon, and is in awe of the beast: its two heads, seven fists, horns raging, but lying quiet and still, defeated by his own blood. He realises that of all the beasts he had fought, none were as awesome and huge as this one – for a second, he realises the awesome power of the gods, and how insignificant he must be – that although he has defeated deities, he has never really taken on any of the powerbrokers – and with a shudder realises he could never have taken Minos, as he rashly thought to Oenone, or a powerful god, as he bragged to the Ferryman – and then a cold sweat breaks out as he must attempt to defeat Neptune...even with Neptune's own power on his side, flowing through him with Jupiter-angering strength, he could not defeat a deity of power, and now he must tackle Neptune's own strength without his power base, and he fears that this whole series of events is merely to awaken another deity of power, as Venus returns to add more strength, more power, and more malice to the gods' omnipotence.

He hears a scream.

He quickens his pace.

The horizon is still beyond him.

The scream contains a darkness, an anger at the world: as the twilight begins, finally, to descend into gloom, he can see the darkness spreading slowly from over the hill, from the direction of the scream.

The expression of anguish haunts him: it appears to have a musical quality, as its pitch begins to resonate, and he feels his breath pounding forth from him like a beat, and his heart's exertions meet with this beat, and act like bass, and wind rushing past his ears creates a sonic flood, and he can hear a song emerging from the mess.

He begins to feel sick: maybe from the run, but maybe from the music. As he begins to feel sick, the music becomes clearer, louder, and increases his sickness. He doubles up in pain, and finds his vision cloudy, but through the dusk he can see his hand.

The Mark is gone.

He fights past the pain and makes his way to the top of the hill, following the gruesome trail of blood. There: in the gloom. He runs towards the sound of crying anguish, his heart stopping at every beat (each one forces blood around: then constricts with such force he fears the next will not come: but with effort, and pain, it does), bile rising in his throat, worry seeping from every pore of his existence, he sees Aricie there, cradling a...a something...

'Where is my son?'

Aricie's scream ends, but the tears flow, and he can hear her sobs up close now, and they are rhythmical, another beat in the sickening song that Theseus can hear. Then: the dawning comprehension.

Twilight becomes darkness, so completely, as Theseus' understanding spreads itself through his being, his gloaming becoming searing. What Aricie cradles is his son, is the mangled body of Aneurin, so tortuously butchered upon the rocks, and Aricie slides away from the corpse, consumed with grief, and

Aneurin's body slips slightly, and then Theseus sees the Mark inscribed on the corpse, cut in by the rocks.

His heart breaks. The grief and guilt are overwhelming: he was too late to save his son from Neptune, whom he had sent after his son in the first place.

He cradles his son in his arms, and he looks down on the broken body, and he sees all the beauty of his son, and he sees it all broken through violence, but that the beauty of his soul shines forth even more strongly because he's broken.

He realises it's the ones who are cracked that the light shines through: and the light of his beauty shines through the cracks of violence, and something strange happens with this realisation.

He can actually hear music.

He looks between Aneurin and Aricie, and realises that he cradles in his arms a being who died thinking he was a rejected lover, and that this being has a beauty that is violence, and finally, in the darkness of his overdue comprehension, the gesamkunstwerk's words make sense.

The melding of beauty and violence is before him. The solo of which the Ferryman spoke was not a rape, it was not in Aneurin nor Phèdre nor himself, but instead the solo is the whole tale in all its orgy of miscommunication which plays the tragedy so beautifully violently, so violently beautiful, as Theseus discovers what the future holds for rejected lovers, and it is beautiful: and finally, Theseus hears the music, as an audible gesamkunstwerk sweeps into existence, and Aricie can hear it too, as strings mournfully echo desperation, and the sound of a thousand voices combine in harmonic disappointment, and there is a bass line which communicates only miscommunication, for this is a gesamkunstwerk more beautiful then the First Movement that plays besides the Styx, for the violence in our world blends its impurities upon the beauty of the song, and a perfection is created as the sight before Theseus is added to his cries of grief mixed with Aricie's sobs, multiplied by the combined heartbreak, and the perfection wends its way into the audible gesamkunstwerk, transforming it with an unexpected solo that is jaw-grinding, awesomely powerful, epically melancholic, and utterly devoid of hope...

epilogue

Listening to the same music, the Ferryman shed a tear.
He spoke one single word in Essil into the darkness. ††††
A thousand souls rose up, and he ferried them across. Now that
the gesamkunstwerk had finished its solo of awesome beauty,
the only unexpected solo in the history of the gesamkunstwerk,
in its eternity-encompassing existence, now that the damned in
the Well of Souls had endured the tragic beauty of the solo, they
flocked from the purgatorial Well into the afterlife. He ferried
them across, and he knew them all.

And yet he did not see Phèdre, nor Aneurin. He did not feel
them in the Well. The music told him that they were not there:
they were not present in this world.

He heard something in the music. It took him an infinity of
ages to realise what it was, and what it meant. Souls had returned
from him before, in epic tales. But he knew there could be no
return from where they were.

Phèdre and Aneurin were bound within their own space,
enduring an eternal torture. Naked, and sweaty, they endured
each other: made to love for the existence of the ages, they

coupled endlessly, eternally. And as they made love, it was a restless affair: Phèdre endured such emotional torture, as she swelled with guilt and self-loathing even as her lust forced her onwards in the continuation of their degradement. Aneurin himself was locked in physical illness, his stomach churning with disgust as he found himself endlessly on top of his stepmother, endlessly invading her against his will, against and in tortured conjunction with her will, endlessly enduring their infinity of torture. No music played for their eternity: an eternity of endurance, as their disgust spread out, but they could not help it, for in the hell created for them they were made to make love, an eternity of restlessness, of awkwardness, an eternity of sweaty self-disgust with no music, no climax, and no forgiveness.

<u>Appendix A: Essil</u>

(gratified for the research by Sp. (Iny) Norman)

† Essil on
    Essil on erifet al
(Pronunciation: ee-sile on [long "i," as in "hi" and long "o" as in "throw"], er-o-fet all)

Literal Translation:
I travelled through light
I travelled through light; I am not afraid

   In Essilian mythology, the pre-gods civilisation, light was the source of everything. People were born of light and remained immortal as long as they upheld nature and light. The preferred communication of scholars and monks was thought and telepathy, which they understood as the pathway of light that bound the minds of all. But for the sake of posterity, they recorded their thoughts in Essil, the language named for light itself.

Their belief was that water preserved light, and from this preservation of light they came into being. They sing an account of their sort of birth, "ete tas Essilev,"... instead of reproduction and natural child-birth, the people of this culture claimed to come into existence from the water and light. The verb "essil" is a concept of both birth and thought. The speaker is talking about swimming in the water before birth, a collection of light and souls (or, arguably, a single soul shared by all). The form "E(e)ssil on" is a first person perfect form of the verb. Our understanding of the perfect form has changed over time. Instead of a single action in the past, the perfect tense here is understood to mean a continuous action... this soul was floating and travelling from the beginning of time, and is still a part of their "essil."

The alternate line's "erifet al" is a first person negative present of the verb "rifet," which means not simply to fear, but to be incredibly fearful, to be terrified. Why would one consider birth fearful in the first place?. The present here, too, is not to be taken in its true form. Rather, it means the person was not afraid at birth, nor are they now. The explanation of this is the Essilian culture considered coming into existence and existence as the same thing, a continuing and never-ending process. So where does fear come in? The Essilians are doing two things: first, they are praising light, Essil, for its comfort and power, but secondly, the speaker is asserting his belief in Essil... therefore he is speaking of his trust that he will continue existence and not be revoked his life (a thought expressed in the noun/infinitive "ocente").

Taking all this in mind, a poetic translation becomes more possible. But, for the sake of the original scheme, it is necessary that its simple repetition and ideology be preserved. Thus the poetic translation:

In this lake of souls
In this lake of souls, I lose all fear.

††

Thanks again to Sp. (Iny) Norman for his invaluable assistance translating the text.

Viðrar vel til loftárása, niðurlæging.

The literal translation is:

Welcome to this place, new being.

Although the poetic translation has been recorded as:

From this damned lake, you will rise.

†††

ág gaf ykkur von sem, varð að vonbrigðum. Petta er ágæntis byrjun.

The only possible translation is:

We have made this sound, but are not happy. This is just a good beginning.

††††

The one word the Ferryman spoke in Essil is unrecordable, for it contains all the poetry of the world. (See Borges' *The Mirror and the Mask*.) All those who hear it can understand, but are bound never to repeat it, lest they multiply the abomination. (Like mirrors and fatherhood, which beget in grotesque ways.) The Ferryman is attempting to fuse the poetry of the world with the gesamkunstwerk, but all those who heard it understood its two meanings in Essil: the first, the literal translation: The Tragedy Has Played, And it Was Beautiful; the second, the poetic translation: The Death Has Come, We Await Meaning. It only takes a small amount of erudition to discover that in this interpretation of the Ferryman's one word that his thoughts focus upon Beauty and Power. He realises that Beauty is all about unlearned privilege and power, and that it is unearned and undeserved as well. He believes that natural Beauty is diabolical as it is destructive, and self-destructive: but that Beauty that is earned – earned the only way possible, through violence, and suffering, and depression – is about as perfect as is possible, and that there must be some happiness in that.

It has been recorded that this is why the Ferryman smiles when he realises where Aneurin and Phèdre are to spend eternity.

B

Appendix B: The House Of Asterion

Every nine years nine men enter the house so that I may deliver them from all evil. I hear their steps or their voices in the depths of the stone galleries and I run joyfully to find them. The ceremony lasts a few minutes. They fall one after another without my having to bloody my hands. They remain where they fell and their bodies help distinguish one gallery from another. I do not know who they are, but I know that one of them prophesied, at the moment of his death, that some day my redeemer would come. Since then my loneliness does not pain me, because I know my redeemer lives and he will finally rise above the dust. If my ear could capture all the sounds of the world, I should hear his steps. I hope he will take me to a place with fewer galleries and fewer doors. What will my redeemer be like?, I ask myself. Will he be a bull or a man? Will he perhaps be a bull with the face of a man? Or will he be like me?

The morning sun reverberated from the bronze sword. There was no longer even a vestige of blood.

'Would you believe it, Ariadne?' said Theseus. 'The Minotaur scarcely defended himself.'

C

Appendix C: The Mark Of Neptune

The Mark of Neptune is a divine sign which endows the bearer, or marker, with the favour of Neptune, commonly regarded as the second most powerful of gods behind Jupiter. It can only be called down by the Champion of Neptune, one whom Neptune has tested and found to be worthy. Although scholarly debate surrounds the issue, it is believed that Neptune openly displays his affinity with humankind in order to anger Jupiter, for he is the only god who has used their ability to Mark humans with favour. The other gods live in fear of provoking Jupiter's wrath.

However, the employment of the Mark is rare, and only three recorded cases have been found in the Library of Babel prior to events recounted here. The first, the earliest recording – dating back some 2,500 years – was found in Justus Perthes' *Historia Naturalis* (written, of course, in Essil.) In this, Perthes recounts the story of Qar, King of Cedron, and the fatalities that result from the Mark.

As the King did not have an heir, who was drowned off the shores of Endis, it is the custom in Cedron that every year the King invites the young men of the land to come before him, and challenge him in mortal combat for the throne. However, they first had to prove themselves by performing three tasks of strength: so far, no-one had been able to complete the tasks since Qar himself, who had the strength of the gods with him as Champion of Neptune.

Near Endis though lived Phoenix, a poor orphan boy who served in the stables. When he reached the age of maturity, fourteen, he set off to Cedron to challenge Qar, as he had fallen in love with Sciénta, Qar's daughter, and desired her for himself. That night he prayed to the gods for the strength, and as he slept in the stables with the horses, Neptune took pity on him, and endowed him with the Mark upon his sword. Unbeknown to Phoenix, he was Qar's heir, presumed drowned. The morning came, and Phoenix entered the Palace, his sword on his back, and strode forth among the potentials, but he was the only man who could complete Qar's tasks. Phoenix caught glimpses of Sciénta, and each made his heart swell with passion.

As was tradition, Qar fought with Phoenix before the masses. Phoenix, however, was massively strong, and although they both shared Neptune's power, Phoenix was younger, and after several hours, Phoenix dealt Qar a mortal blow. As he lay dying, Sciénta ran out to him, and from on close she saw Phoenix's blade, and saw upon it the Mark: and she knew that Phoenix was Qar's son, and Qar saw this with his last breath as he died at his son's hands. Phoenix understood this too, and wept at his father's death, and as Sciénta cried, he realised his crime, and the incestuous nature of his love, and impaled himself on his sword. The Mark was not found on his sword, but as the priests dressed Phoenix for burial, they found the Mark on his skin. It was not burnt on, nor cut: they were at a loss to explain its appearance, and thought that it was an unusual birthmark. Only Sciénta, who recognised it from the sword, had the presence of mind to record it for posterity, as Perthes includes a diagram.

Holinshed's *Chronicle* records that the second instance of the Mark occurred in the Kingdom of Byrrum approximately one thousand years ago. King Helax discovered that his wife, the beautiful temptress Queen Salomith, was engaged in an adulterous affair with Eyron, a young warrior of the court. Helax was a good leader, and had surrounded himself with faithful, learned men, one of whom – Opelle – was his favourite. Opelle had read Perthes' account of Phoenix and the Mark, and he told Helax he could call upon Neptune's power to endow the Mark upon his sword so he could slay Eyron. This Helax did, and Neptune obeyed his request, and the Mark once again shone bright on a sword. However, Helax was betrayed: Salomith discovered the plot, and seduced Opelle (an otherwise upstanding citizen), and while he was sleeping, she took the sword with the Mark upon it and threw it in the furnace, where it melted.

The next day the appointed time for the duel came. Helax, although the inferior warrior, was confident of victory through Neptune's power. However, when he arrived on the battlefield, he discovered his sword was missing, and his second-in-command Opelle realised that he had been betrayed. Helax determinedly fought Eyron, hoping that love would be enough, but Eyron slew Helax effortlessly.

His world broken, and consumed with guilt and a jealous lust, Opelle stole from the shadows surrounding Eyron and Salomith's celebrations and slew the Queen in the brightness of the victory. Eyron, enraged, killed Opelle, but was then cursed by Neptune with an empty, immortal life: he travelled the world for eight hundred years, looking for the River of Death which would bring an end to his immortality, but after eight hundred years of searching, he had experienced everything that humanity had to offer, and he retired to a cave in the land of Canai, where legend has it he still waits, in grief, for the end of the world.

This second instance of the Mark is perhaps the most important when we attempt to plot the development of the Mark. As a result of Salomith's deception, the Mark was destroyed, and Neptune was angered greatly. He cursed Eyron in his rage, and swore that his Mark would never again be destroyed: from now on, the one who invokes the curse would have the Mark on their body until their purpose is completed, so that the curser's life is forfeit unless they complete their task. Upon the moment that death is physically assured, that neither modern medicine nor the intrusion of another god can save them, the Mark is instantaneously transferred from the curser to the cursed, so with their dying moments they can know that Neptune has killed them.

And so the third, and last, recorded case (in Fumes' *Memorious*) of the Mark of Neptune begins with King Pläs of Athens, three hundred years ago. He had two sons, Estan and Estle, of which Estle was his favourite. Although Estan was the eldest, and a powerfully strong man, when Estle reached his fourteenth birthday, Pläs declared that Estle would rule after his death. Angered, Estan called on Neptune's power, and was surprised that the Mark was inscribed on his flesh. It burned bright, and he felt its awesome power. Coursing with Neptune's power, he caught Estle unaware, and was about to strike him down when Neptune tested him, and the Mark glowed bright, began to bleed, and Estan, proving himself unworthy, screamed out in pain. Estle was alerted, and fled to a safe location – the Vault of the Gods, in the grounds of the royal palace, where even then (perhaps since before time?) an omnipotent presence lies within music. Estan chased him there, but knew he could not enter, for the music would smite him. A wait ensued as Estan laid siege to Estle, but Neptune is cruel, and angry that Estan was not worthy, and the sound of the waves upon the shore lulled Estan to sleep. Estle emerged from the Vault and saw Estan asleep: he cut his throat in the night.

Although Neptune was satisfied with Estan's death – to him, it was a corpse bearing the Mark, and that was enough – Estle feared that it was only time before Neptune came to him to smite him. He was correct: Neptune is an impatient god. However, Estle was aware that the Mark can only be called by a Champion of Neptune, or one of his blood. He realised that if he married outside royal blood, in the eyes of the court and the gods, he was no longer of royal blood. In essence, through marriage to Cleoné (his love and a simple court musician) he died as Estle, son of Pläs, tied to a royal line and an affinity with Neptune, and would be reborn as Estle, husband to Cleoné. In this way, the Mark is gone and Neptune is satisfied.

Since the discovery of Perthes' text, and of subsequent references in other texts in the Library of Babel, such as Holinshed's *Chronicle* and Fumes' *Memorious*, Champions of Neptune have made a point of educating themselves and their kin in the language of Essil and the history of the Mark. However, the tragic nature of the Mark – all who have used it are betrayed by it – means it has gone unused since the strong Prince Estle of Athens, as Champions are fearful that they are too weak to control the Mark.

However, it was Borges' recent investigation into Essil and the workings of the Mark that influenced modern thinking about the Mark. (See *The Immortal and the Mark.*) His densely philosophical but immaculately crafted work hypothesised that if the Mark is invoked by the Champion of Neptune disaster would occur, except if they charged Neptune himself with the action required. In this way, there would be no betrayal of the Champion, nor their request. Neptune would be left to his own free will, and as such he will act without human involvement, which Borges understood caused instabilities and imperfection by definition.

It is almost certain that Theseus and Aneurin, who could both speak Essil, were completely aware of the Mark's history, and had read Borges' hypothesis on the future of the Mark.